Love is
a time of enchantment:
in it all days are fair and all fields
green. Youth is blest by it,
old age made benign:
the eyes of love see
roses blooming in December,
and sunshine through rain. Verily
is the time of true-love
a time of enchantment — and
Oh! how eager is woman
to be bewitched!

TAKE NOW, PAY LATER

A bi-sexual king (James I); his handsome, red-haired favourite; a beautiful, blonde, married countess; a dark, bad-tempered diplomat; a conniving go-between; homosexuality; deceit; adultery; divorce; poison; murder and imprisonment are the ingredients of a seventeenth-century scandal which shook most of Europe in its day. This fiction based on fact is the love-turning-to-hate story of Robert Carr, Earl of Somerset, and his wife, Frances.

Books by Joanna Dessau
Published by The House of Ulverscroft:

THE GREY GOOSE
THE BLACKSMITH'S DAUGHTER
CROWN OF SORROWS
NO WAY OUT
THE CONSTANT LOVER

JOANNA DESSAU

TAKE NOW,
PAY LATER

Complete and Unabridged

ULVERSCROFT
Leicester

First Large Print Edition
published 1997

British Library CIP Data

Dessau, Joanna
    Take now, pay later.—Large print ed.—
Ulverscroft large print series: romance
    1. English fiction—20th century
    2. Large type books
    I. Title
823.9′14 [F]

ISBN 0-7089-3715-2

Published by
F. A. Thorpe (Publishing) Ltd.
Anstey, Leicestershire

Set by Words & Graphics Ltd.
Anstey, Leicestershire
Printed and bound in Great Britain by
T. J. Press (Padstow) Ltd., Padstow, Cornwall

This book is printed on acid-free paper

To

PETER ELMSLIE

With my love.

Acknowledgements

My grateful thanks and acknowledgements to:

The Administrator and Assistants, Greys Court, Rotherfield Greys, Oxfordshire.
Miss S. J. Barnes, County Archivist, Oxfordshire County Council.
Ms. Rosemary Evison, Archive Assistant, The National Portrait Gallery, London.
John Murdoch Esq., The Victoria & Albert Museum, London.
David Setford Esq., Curator, The Watford Museum, Watford, Herts.

1

THE FALLEN IDOL.

Greys Court, Oxfordshire.

1632

THE afternoon sun slanted in through the leaded window panes of an upper room in the handsome hilltop mansion of Greys Court, some two or three miles westerly of Henley-on-Thames. The sick woman, propped up on a mound of pillows behind the looped-back tapestry curtains of a great four-poster bed, gazed dully at the bright dancing motes of a sunbeam, noting listlessly how the light, where it fell upon the satin counterpane, seemed to brighten the crimson to scarlet. The pain struck again and she cried out.

An attendant hurried to the bedside, raised the woman's head and gave her a draught. "It will ease the pain, my Lady," she said. "The doctors have promised it."

"Nothing eases it, Dorothy," whispered the Countess of Somerset, her head falling back against the lace-trimmed pillows. "'Tis dulled but for a little while only, and then — " She sighed and moved restlessly. "I would I might die and be out of it all, but even that is not vouchsafed me. I must suffer and suffer again."

Grey-haired Dorothy Badby stared down at her mistress, her round face impassive. Ay, she thought, suffer you should, for you have richly deserved it; no one more so. It is God's retribution on you, for sure, such trouble have you wrought, my Lady. Who would credit, thought Dorothy Badby, gazing upon the face of her mistress, that this wretched creature had once been the desire of many men, considered one of the beauties of her day? Looking at the sunken, dark-circled eyes, the hollow cheeks and temples, the mouth stretched tight over teeth brought into sudden prominence by extreme emaciation, the once creamy skin blotched and sallow,

2

the once beautiful golden hair now dry and sparse, Dorothy shook her head in reluctant sympathy. In truth, it was terrible to die so, in long-drawn-out agony, hideous, unwanted, unloved, rejected by those who had courted her. Even my Lady's husband wished naught to do with her and never visited her, for all she loved him to distraction.

Why, when she had still been able to stand, my Lady had stayed ever at her window, watching for my Lord to go by. Only the merest glimpse of him would she gain if he happened to walk in the gardens, but she would smile and sigh and sob like a young girl looking upon her first lover. He never gave any signal, never glanced up, never came to her room, nor sent her any note, nor had he spoken one word to her since their release from the Tower of London ten years earlier. All his love had turned to an immovable hatred, for he blamed her for all the misfortunes that had come upon him, seeming to mislike so much as to breathe the same air as his wife.

My Lord was still handsome enough to turn any woman's head, reflected

Dorothy, seating herself on a stool and taking up her sewing. To her mind, he was better looking now than he had been when King James had first clapped eyes on him all those years ago. There had been a softness, a prettiness about his looks then which had appealed mightily to His Majesty, but now my Lord's face, though thin, sad and weary, had a firmness and strength about it that had been missing before his imprisonment. Dorothy thought it an improvement, but who cared for her opinion? Assuredly not my Lord. He who had once strutted, a very popinjay, clad in silks, satins and jewellery, now paid no heed to what he wore or how he appeared, caring only for the Lady Anne, his seventeen year old daughter by the Countess, a daughter he knew only from her letters and a portrait.

'Tis amazing what we come to, considered Dorothy. Here lies my Lady, whom I have known and served since her petted, indulged childhood as daughter of the leading noble family of England, here she lies, dying in lonely misery at the age of thirty-nine, while I, but a serving woman, am sound in health and wits at the age of fifty-two. Sure, money and rank do not bring happiness or my Lord would still be as mad for my Lady as he was in earlier days, when they were young and thought the world their plaything.

"Dorothy," croaked the hoarse voice from the bed, "Dorothy, does my Lord walk in the garden? Go to the window and see. Tell me if he be there. Does he look up? Does he?"

Shrugging her shoulders, Dorothy laid aside her needlework, rose from the stool and walked to the window overlooking the small formal garden with its neat flower-beds cut into geometrical shapes and separated by gravel walks that converged upon a fountain whose dancing spray jetted high in the sunny air, falling in a multitude of crystalline droplets.

"No," she said. "No one is there, my Lady."

Nor will be, she thought. Nor ever will be, for he hates the very notion of you.

"But 'tis a lovely day, Doll," came the weak voice again. "Bright enough to tempt him out. Art certain he is not there?"

"There is no one," repeated the maid. "Mayhap he is on the castle side of the house, my Lady," she went on, taking pity on the dying woman. "'Tis the side he prefers. He likes to wander among the ruins and the shade from the trees is pleasant, cooler than the gardens on this side. Rest assured, he walks among the ruins."

But he does not, for all that, she mused. Nay, he is withindoors, in some dim chamber, chin on hand, sunk in melancholy, as well I know. For him the sun never shines, except perhaps through the Lady Anne and she is soon to wed. It is a fair match too, considering all, to Lord William Russell, who loves her. This is a glum enough household and I would be well to leave it but for the fact that my heart is wrung with pity for my Lord and Lady, the poor creatures as they have become.

"Dorothy," whispered the Countess, "do you fetch Cecily to sit with me while you go to my Lord . . . Ay, go to him and beg him, implore him, to come to me for a little moment only . . . for the sake of the love he once bore me . . . My eyes ache for the sight of him just once before I die . . . Oh, do not shake your head, good Doll . . . go, I pray you . . . Do, I beseech you, dear Doll."

Sighing, Dorothy went to do her bidding, finding the Earl of Somerset seated in the winter parlour, elbows on a table, head in hands. Hearing the door open and the rustle of footsteps in the rushes, he looked up, large blue eyes clouded, full mouth flattened and drawn down, red stubble about his unshaven chin, red hair lank and unkempt upon his broad shoulders.

"Yes?" he queried listlessly. Then sharply: "What do you want? Is it news of my daughter?"

Dorothy curtsied. "Nay, my Lord. The Lady Anne is very well, I believe. 'Tis my Lady Countess — " She paused as a look of weary distaste passed over his face, then, pressing bravely on: " — 'tis that the Countess wishes your company desperate bad, sir. She longs to see you but once before she dies."

"She is dying then? You speak truth?"

"I speak truth, my Lord. She cannot

last above a day or two more. The doctors have told me so and indeed, it is plain to see."

He seemed, without moving, to shrink into himself. "It is of no use," he said. "It was good of you to bring the message, but I shall not go. It is of no use."

"But, sir!" protested Dorothy, shocked. "It is her dying wish. Oh, you cannot refuse her dying wish, my Lord."

"I do refuse it," he answered expressionlessly. "I shall not go, think of me what you will." Seeing the woman's face, he was stung into unwilling explanation. "Hark ye!" he exclaimed with sudden force, flinging up his head. "If I go, if I so much as lay eyes on her, I am like to strangle her with my own hands and send her to her Maker before her appointed time. If I am to go to the devil, I would go to him with these hands unstained with the blood of another, with my conscience light of a murder, whatever else I may have or have not done. Who can say the same of her who lies upstairs? Now, begone and trouble me no more with this matter. Tell your mistress that I will pray for her if I can bring myself to do so. That is all."

Rising from his chair, he walked with a slouching step across the room and out of another door, banging it behind him, climbing the stair with dragging feet to the Long Gallery, where he paced moodily up and down, his thoughts confused, heavy with regret, wild with frustration, dark with despair.

"Oh God!" he cried suddenly to the sunlit empty space of the great room. "Oh God, that I was born a fool! How could I have been so blind, so half-witted, so puffed up with my own importance that I saw and understood nothing — *nothing*? Why did I not pay heed to Tom? And there is no one to blame but myself for my conceit. I would wed her — I would do it! I thought it fine to treat His Majesty with boredom and contempt; the King who is now dead and who was always so good to me, no matter if he — ah, do not think of it! And, oh Tom, poor Tom, if you are in Heaven, look down and forgive me, for I cannot forgive myself!"

Flinging himself down on a cushioned settle, he wept as he had done so often, for the innocent, good-hearted boy he had been, for the position of power he had been given; for trust and friendship lost and love turned to hate. Before God, if he had his time over again, how differently would he live it! If he had his time over again, he would stay in his own country of Scotland, no matter what, and never set foot in cruel England, Kings, wealth, rank and power notwithstanding. His life was a desert, a weary grey wilderness, but for the daughter he had never seen, the bright and lovely Lady Anne Carr. From what he knew of her from her letters and her portrait, she had inherited his looks, but not his thick headpiece, the good Lord be praised! Pray Heaven and all angels that she had naught of her mother. Surely such a misfortune could not be visited upon a guiltless girl! Her mother, 'twas said, had ever been spoiled and wilful, intent upon her own way, uncaring of whom she hurt, nor of how many lies she told to gain it. Well, she had got her way, which was to wed him — and see where it had brought them! To disgrace, imprisonment, ruin and misery.

Ah, Anne could not be like her mother!

Nay, he was sure she was not and nor must Lord William Russell be who was soon to wed her. His family had not cared for the match and no wonder, but it seemed that Lord William had fallen in love with Anne, and the Earl of Somerset, her father, shamed and under house-arrest as he was, must be grateful for that. He would pray God for her happiness when she became Lady Anne Russell, so sweet as he was assured she was, so truthful, so loving, such as he himself had been once, long ago, when all the world was beautiful and kind, or so he had thought in his boyish innocence.

So long ago.

He shut his eyes remembering, his heart aching for what might have been . . .

★ ★ ★

As youngest son of the dead Laird of Ferniehurst Castle, a few miles south of Jedburgh in the Border Country of Scotland, he had been sent to the Royal Household in Edinburgh as a page, back in 1600, through the influence of his father's friends and had made a sorry mull of it. Of course, he had never been overly gifted with brains, recalled the Earl with a twisted half-smile. Had enough ado to read and write, let alone to know the meaning of Latin! It was unlucky, therefore, that King James VI of Scotland, as His Majesty had been then, was a remarkable scholar in all subjects, especially Latin, for this had been the cause of the young Robert Kerr being sent home under a cloud.

What a noodle he had made of himself, that day at Court in Edinburgh! He had been fortunate enough to be taken there as page to the Earl of Dunbar, for he was of excellent family and his widowed mother had fully expected him to do well. Alas for her fond expectations! He had made himself a laughing-stock instead.

Why, in the name of Heaven had Lord Dunbar chosen him, the fourteen year old Robert Kerr, to read the Latin grace at dinner upon that misfortunate day in Edinburgh? He had protested to my Lord, but his patron had brushed these objections genially aside.

"Go to, Robbie!" he had laughed. "Ye'll get through it well enough, ma laddie. His Majesty will be too taken up wi' lookin' at yer pretty face tae ken what ye read!"

Lord Dunbar had been wrong. King James, always ready to be well disposed to a handsome youngster, had beamed upon him, but at the first few tortured sounds that had issued from Robert's perfectly chiselled lips, his indulgent smile had changed to an expression of dismay as the boy's tongue refused to curl itself round the syllables that were so foreign and so incomprehensible to its owner.

"Och, this is naught but gibberish!" had cried agonised Majesty, jumping to his feet. "I canna stand it. Be silent, laddie and get yersel' oot o' here quick. Go hame an' dinna return till ye've got yer Latin! Be off wi' ye!"

So Robert had been sent home to Ferniehurst, a sad failure.

"Eh, Robbie, what'll we do wi' ye?" had wailed Madam Kerr in despair. "To lose such a fine place and yersel' but a youngest son! If yer father were only alive, he could help ye, for sure. 'Twas through the memory o' his friendship wi' the King's friend, the Duke of Lennox, that ye got the position, for His Majesty is loyal to his friends and his friend's friends, ye ken. We'll have tae think o' somewhat else for ye, there's nae help for it, I'm thinking. I'll speak tae yer uncle and see what he can do. Meanwhile, ye must amuse yersel' aboot the place as best ye may. Take that young English friend of yours aboot a little and show him our countryside."

Robert's young English friend was a certain Thomas Overbury, second son of Sir Nicholas Overbury of Bourton-on-the-Hill in Gloucestershire, who had been sent by his knightly father on a holiday of pleasure and had met Robert Kerr, then page to the Earl of Dunbar, in Edinburgh. Tiring of Edinburgh, Thomas had decided to visit Ferniehurst Castle and renew his friendship with Robert. Now nineteen years old, dark, handsome, tall and well-made, Overbury was awesomely intelligent and had determined on a diplomatic career, this holiday being given him by his father to enjoy before he began life in earnest. The young man found Robert amusing and attractive, despite his lack of book-learning. There was a directness, a warm-hearted generosity about the boy that was most appealing to one of Thomas Overbury's cool and calculating nature, not to mention his good looks which also appealed, for Overbury's tastes lay rather more with men than with women, although Robert had no idea of this, being innocent and ingenuous to a degree that was child-like, even infantile. Indeed, so guileless was Master Robert that he was quite unaware of the thoughts and feelings of those with whom he lived.

Tall and strongly made for his fourteen years, long-legged and broad-shouldered, with a mass of long, waving, coppery hair, haughty aristocratic features, large blue eyes and a firm, chiselled mouth, he was a sight to make any young maid's heart beat faster, but as yet he had no interest in the opposite sex, being beguiled only by hunting, riding, shooting with the bow and arrow and such artless sports.

"Robbie, thou'rt nothing but an ignoramus!" had teased Tom Overbury one fine day as they walked through the garden on the way to fish in Jedwater Stream that flowed nearby. "Art wholly without cunning that you notice nothing of good or evil in what men say and do?"

"Well, I have noticed that ye have come to Ferniehurst to stay awhile wi' me in ma disgrace," Robert had replied, laughing. "And I notice, too, that ye're far from an ignoramus yersel', Tom. Wheesht, man, ye're nigh as learned as our King Jamie, to ma mind! It must be grand to have such a headpiece, ay, grand indeed. I fear that mine is as thick as a block or as empty as a drum, choose which ye will! O' course," he went on, struck by a thought, "ye're older than I by some years which might mak' a difference, eh? After all, ye have nineteen years to ma fourteen."

Tom forebore to remind Robert that he himself had matriculated from Oxford University at the tender age of fourteen, merely smiling quietly. "Oh," he said, "with your looks you won't be in disgrace for long, I'll warrant. I hear that Sir James Hay has noticed you and wishes to have you with him."

"What!" had cried Robert, amazed. "Sir James Hay, the King's friend? But I made such a ninny o' masel' — he saw and heard the King rebuke me. What can Sir James want wi' me?"

A peculiar expression flickered over Tom Overbury's face. "I wonder if I should tell you?" he murmured. "I fear to shatter your pristine innocence."

The two had seated themselves on the river bank, the sun shining bright overhead, birdsong filling the clear air. Robert moved closer to his friend.

"Shatter ma innocence? Why, what mean ye, Tom?"

Tom had shrugged and cast a pebble into the fast-moving water, watching the rings it made widen and fade, before he answered. "Sir James Hay has a fondness for pretty boys."

"I see," answered Robert, who did not see at all. "So he has chosen me. That is most kind."

"Swounds!" Tom shook his head at such obtuseness. "Kind, you call it? Many would not! I think he means to make a pet of you, Robbie; to favour you; to — dear me, must I catalogue it all?"

17

"Och, I dinna ken yer meaning." Robert's blue eyes were puzzled and enquiring. "Ye'd best say all ye have in mind, I'm thinking."

"He may wish to make you his minion. Dear God!" cried Tom, seeing Robert still uncomprehending. "That is French for *mignon*, which, in English, means 'darling'. *Now* do you understand? His plaything, his catamite! Robert I beg of you, do not goggle at me like a zany! He — may — wish — to — bed — you!" roared Tom, with a pause between each shouted word.

"But — but — I am a boy!" Robert had stammered, astounded. "How can he bed me?"

"Christ Jesus have mercy!" Tom slapped his forehead and rolled his eyes heavenward at such idiocy. "He can, oh, he can, believe me! And unless you are mighty spry, he may well do so. The Court of your Scottish King is notorious for such goings-on. You have dwelt there. Have you not heard or seen?"

"Nay," said Robert blankly. "I thought all to be gallant and merry."

"Ay," nodded Tom. "And I daresay,"

he observed drily, "that you would not notice if someone thrust a lance up your backside."

At this, Robert burst into a laugh. "Och, Tom, ye're such a joker! Why, I'm right handy wi' a lance and can give good account of maself in the tilt-yard. Jousting is one thing I can do well!"

Tom Overbury stared at his young friend, quite disconcerted. Was it possible for anyone to be so naïve, so imperceptive? Jesu, but it seemed so. He was glad that he had carried his feelings of attraction no further than friendship, for to have shown young Kerr his true desires would, of a surety, have caused a devilish scandal at Ferniehurst, with Robert horrified, Mistress Kerr outraged — for her son would doubtless have blabbed all to her — and Thomas Overbury cast out of the comfortable castle in vile disfavour, which would have not been at all to his liking. Overbury was not one to parade his sexual proclivities for all to see; he may have preferred men, but did not disdain a woman, if one was to his fancy. He knew how to keep himself to himself. So this bird would not fly.

His shoulders lifted in a slight shrug. Hey-day, there were others. The world was wide and he was on a holiday of pleasure. As for Robert Kerr, he would have to take his chance. Tom had tried to warn him, but it was clear that the lad was one who would have to learn by experience.

★ ★ ★

In the Long Gallery of Greys Court, Lord Somerset shifted on the settle. He was only forty-six, but already rheumatism had him by the heels at times, a legacy from his imprisonment in the Tower, where no one could escape the damp and chill, be he lodged ever so comfortable therein. He shifted again. Lord, but his knees ached like the devil! Ay, he remembered those old Ferniehurst days well. Too well for his peace of mind, he feared. His childlike innocence had been tarnished soon enough. He had gone with Sir James Hay in his entourage to France and there had remained for several years. He had seen, he had learned and had been greatly surprised by the knowledge

20

he had gained. Nor had he come away entirely unscathed and uncorrupted, for he had been forced to understand, at last, what Tom Overbury had been trying to tell him by the river upon that day at Ferniehurst. He had escaped too much personal experience, however, discovering that, if given the chance, he was sexually attracted to women and not to men.

Oh God, what a fool I was! thought the Earl, moving restlessly. Mayhap it was because my father had died in the year of my birth, leaving me to be brought up by my mother — who knows? But I was always a dunce — I was fashioned that way . . .

He rose stiffly, with a groan, wandering to a window, gazing out unseeing at the green and gold of the sunlit beech trees, at the ragged shapes of the ruined mediaeval castle across the courtyard, from which much of Greys Court had been built. Would I could live my time over again! Oh God, how different, how very different would I be!

Yet stay, would I be so different? he wondered. Mayhap Fate had decreed that my life should run as I have lived it,

21

so that do as I would, all would be the same? That I would be lifted from gentlemanly obscurity to be first noble in the land, that I should love and wed the most beautiful lady, have riches, power, position, and lose all, to end as I am now. Who can tell?

So my wife is dying. Welladay, she is well out of it and I wish that God may forgive her, for I cannot. Would I might die too and end this life that is naught but bitter dust and ashes to me, Earl of Somerset, fallen idol.

2

HOW IT ALL BEGAN.

1607

THE weather was kind, though chilly, on King's Day, the 24th of March 1607, in London, with a bright sun and a keen wind. The tourney, held in the tilt-yard of Whitehall Palace, was about to begin amid a continuous hum of laughter and chatter as the gaily clad squires presented the shields of their lords to the King.

King James VI of Scotland, now also James I of England, was seated in a carved and gilded chair, his wife, the vivacious Danish blonde Queen Anne, beside him in a smaller chair, beneath an especially constructed shelter in the centre of one of the decorated stands. The Queen, magnificently attired in a sable wrap that had once been the property of Queen Elizabeth Tudor of tremendous memory, a plumed purple velvet hat upon her golden head, was talking animatedly to the Countess of Suffolk standing at her side. One of the Countess's daughters, married the year before at the age of thirteen to the Earl of Essex, fidgeted nearby, her pretty babyish face sullen with boredom, despite her mother's nudgings and whisperings to keep still and look pleasant. She was seldom at Court, being deemed too young, but a tourney was felt to be unexceptional and unlikely to corrupt such a youthful lady.

His Majesty, never one for sartorial splendour, was huddled into a fur-lined, hooded, woollen cloak of a plain dark blue, the hood pulled well forward over his ears, he being careful of his health and nervous of catching cold in the searching wind that found its way into the crimson-painted, laurel-decked shelter.

"Och, look there, Philip," he said over his shoulder to one of his favourites, Philip Herbert, Earl of Montgomery, who stood just behind him, "here comes Jamie Hay, the dear mannie. I'm sae glad to have him back from France! Eh, but he looks well in his cloth of gold and white velvet, wi' his blue-clad pages following him." He leaned forward, his interest suddenly caught. "Who's that, Philip? Who's that braw laddie bearing Sir James's shield? Ooh, what a pretty boy!"

The foppish, disdainful Lord Montgomery craned his neck, peering. "I cannot tell, Sire," he replied languidly. "Some country bumpkin, I make no doubt. No one of note, surely."

"He rides well," remarked the King. "Like a bonnie young centaur."

Lord Montgomery shrugged scornful shoulders as the young rider pulled his horse up on the gravel beneath the King's box. As he made to leap to the ground with Sir James Hay's shield, the horse, frightened by a scarf waved too close to its head by an excited lady, shied badly, causing its rider to lose his balance and fall heavily. Lord Montgomery's shout of laughter was drowned by the King's cry of dismay as the boy did not jump to his feet, but lay still and white where he had fallen.

"God's nails! The laddie's hurt!" His Majesty sprang to his feet. "Someone help him — quick, I say!" He leaned over the rail, gazing anxiously down at the motionless figure, as a page hurried to the frightened horse and led it away before its restless hooves could strike and injure the fallen youth still more. There was a further commotion as the King insisted on leaving his place to descend to the gravel of the tilt-yard, where he called for stretcher-bearers and a doctor to come yarely, yarely!

"Puir, puir laddie," murmured King James, staring at the white face as someone placed a cushion beneath the red head, its long waving locks dragging in the dust. "See, 'tis his leg that's twisted. I doubt not that it be broken." His stare grew more intent. "Nay, but I know this boy, surely! 'Tis young Kerr o' Ferniehurst, the one who mixed me such a pickle wi' the Latin grace at Edinburgh! Well, well, and here he is again!" He turned impatiently, beckoning to the stretcher-bearers who were coming at a run, and to his own physician who was bustling forward. "Will ye no' be quick, men? And you, Sir Theodore, do ye examine the laddie at once. 'Tis his

26

leg, puir soul, d'ye see?"

Doctor Sir Theodore Turquet de Mayerne, a tall, plump, handsome Frenchman, the King's personal physician and friend of the royal family, swiftly satisfied himself that Robert Kerr had sustained no further injuries than a broken leg and turned to the King for instructions.

"Where would Your Majesty wish the young man to be taken?" he enquired in excellent English with only a trace of accent. "Is there, perhaps, a person here who could give him accommodation?"

"He may have room in my house," said a quiet gentleman standing near. "It is near to the Cross at Charing, if the King pleases to have him carried there."

"Ma thanks tae ye, Sir Robert Rider! See that the laddie is placed in comfort, will ye? 'Tis good of ye, sir. I'll not forget it."

The King's gratitude seemed somewhat excessive, thought Sir Robert, but it were ever best to keep on the sunny side of those in power and, with any luck, he might get some reward from his action.

Besides, his house was commodious enough and he had servants a-plenty to care for the injured squire who appeared to have taken the Scottish monarch's fancy.

The Scottish monarch's fancy had indeed been taken and to such a degree that he could scarcely give eyes to the tournament, once it had begun. King James, brilliantly intellectual, affectionate, generous and kindly, was bi-sexual and ready, at the age of forty-one, to give his heart to anyone good-hearted and obliging. He had known love for the woman who was his wife, whom he married in 1589, when he had been twenty-three and she fourteen, and had enjoyed the marriage bed sufficiently to give his Queen seven children, of whom three had survived, but the feeling between them had cooled, with time, to an undemanding friendship. He had also had at least two or three extra-marital affairs of short duration, but his emotions could be greatly stirred by a handsome young man, even to the extent of falling deeply in love. Indeed, he had chosen several male favourites during his lifetime, the first being his French cousin, Esmé Stuart, Sieur d'Aubigny, whom he had created Duke of Lennox.

Esmé Stuart had come to Scotland in 1579 as an elegant, good-looking, highly sophisticated man of some twenty years to young King James's thirteen summers. Wholly starved of affection, reared by stern guardians, the orphaned boy-King had conceived a violent hero-worship for his stylish, glamorous, though unscrupulous cousin, who did not repulse him, being amused to pet him and teach him certain practices which James, after initial shock, found exciting enough to become irresistible, so that he fell madly in love with the handsome, over-sexed Sieur d'Aubigny who was already notorious for his lechery amongst women.

Certain it is, that if Esmé Stuart had been a woman, poor James's homosexual instincts might never have been aroused. As it was, he preferred to surround himself with male favourites, one of whom was the resplendent Sir James Hay, later created Earl of Carlisle, another being Philip Herbert, Earl of Montgomery, whose physical beauty was belied by a boorish, drunken, womanising character and whose star was about to fall, had he but known it.

Meanwhile, King James fidgeted in his seat, kicking his twisted foot impatiently against the leg of his chair as he thought about Robert Kerr. Would the tourney never be done?

"Oh hush!" frowned Queen Anne. "You make such a noise that you distract the riders. We have had one accident; is that not enough?"

The King hunched a shoulder and forebore to reply. Should he halt the tourney? Nay, that would be discourteous to those who had arranged it for his pleasure and James was ever gracious in his manners to others. Besides, this was a show after his own heart, not too warlike, for he hated sharp weapons of any kind. It was more like a series of pageants and much thought had obviously been given to its organisation; he must stay to the end, or give great offence to those who had thought to please him. But how was the boy, young Kerr? Och, how deathly he had looked when the bearers had carried him away. And his leg! Suppose it should heal twisted? King James kicked his chair again. Pray God that so straight and beautiful a body be not marred! King James could not endure the thought. Dr. de Mayerne should treat the laddie, ay, and he himself would visit the boy to mark his progress and to discover more of him. The King's heart beat faster and he kicked his chair yet again, to the Queen's manifest annoyance.

At last all was finished; the prizes presented, the riders and horses retired, the stands emptying as the watchers dispersed and His Majesty was free and riding fast for Charing Cross, eager as a green youth galloping to meet his sweetheart.

★ ★ ★

Robert Kerr, recovering consciousness after Dr. de Mayerne had set his leg with cool and skilful hands, lay in the comfortable bed in a luxurious chamber kept for guests in Sir Robert Rider's house and stared about him with dazed blue eyes. He was vaguely aware of having made a botch of things before the

King once again. Sure, his luck was well out. First the Latin grace, now this!

He had no real idea of where he might be, except that he was being treated with as much consideration as though he had won all the prizes in the tourney, instead of having dropped his lord's shield, fallen from his mount and measured his length upon the ground before the eyes of His Majesty and all the Court. Why this tenderness, he could not tell. He turned his head on the pillow. There, at his bedside, was a silver tray holding a jug of some drink and a plate of sweet cakes on a stand, with a small golden bell placed near. It was amazing! Nor could it last, he thought gloomily. He would be turned off, soon enough; there must be some mistake, although what kind of mistake he could not imagine.

As it was, Sir James Hay would be certain to relieve him of his post for this latest blunder. 'Fore God, but his leg hurt! Robert hoped that it would not heal crooked, for it was undoubtedly broken. What wretched fortune. He lay, speculating gloomily on his future, when the door opened and the King came in.

Astonished, Robert tried to raise himself, but the King moved forward rapidly to press him back.

"Na, na, laddie, rest ye. I do but come tae see how ye progress after such a nasty tumble. Your leg be broke, I fear, but good Dr. de Mayerne, ma own leech, has set it. He is a right clever fellow, so ye're in gude hands. And how d'ye feel, eh?"

"Oh — ah — well enough, Sir, I thank ye," stammered Robert, quite at a loss for the reason for such condescension. He stared at the King as that gentleman found himself a chair and lowered himself into it, beaming and nodding encouragingly.

"Sleep if ye wish, ma dearie," he said in his strong Scots brogue. "I dinna mind. I'll watch over ye a wee while."

This was enough to make Robert's drooping lids fly open at once. Sleep? Before His Majesty? Certes, the world was turned upside down this day! But indeed, he did feel mortal tired and, glancing at the King and receiving a smiling nod, he began to relax and soon drifted off to sleep.

A few moments later, King James rose and softly approached the bedside. Lord, what a lovely boy was this Robert Kerr! Stretching out a thin, long-fingered hand, the King brushed the lad's red-gold hair tenderly off his forehead. When he recovers, thought His Majesty, I'll do so much for him, the pretty poppet. I'll make him love me, look to me for everything. He's gently bred, of good family, has travelled abroad, so will not be without social graces. Och, I'm wondering if he's got his Latin yet!

He walked to the window and looked out absently. He was glad that he was a ruler, for few would deny him his wishes. Even if this beautiful laddie inclined to women, he would not refuse his King, especially if his King made it worth his while, surely! Not that he would be punished if he did refuse; James was not vindictive. But oh, he loved beauty in all its forms! And he, who worshipped beauty, was cursed with weak legs and a twisted foot. Well, it was not precisely twisted, but turned far outward, while his legs, though long, were neither strong nor elegantly shaped, caused, folk said, through his mother's terrible experiences when she was pregnant with him.

He had never known a mother's love, for he had no memory of her. He had been taken from her too young for memories, but he had heard enough about her and little of it good. She had been Mary, Queen of Scots, accused of complicity in the murder of her husband, James's father; reviled, captured, immured twenty years in English houses, under permanent arrest, and finally executed by command of his royal predecessor and godmother, Elizabeth Tudor, toward whom he had never borne ill-will. He gave a short sigh. As to that, nor had he ever known a father's love. Unfortunate, unfortunate . . .

Both his parents had been exceptionally tall and exceptionally handsome, by all accounts, whereas he, their son, was of middle height only and of ordinary enough appearance, although he was said to take after his mother somewhat in looks. Judging from the portraits he had seen of her, he had inherited the large sad eyes, the long nose, the small mouth, the oval, high-cheekboned face, but in him all this was transmuted into unremarkable pleasantness only — nothing outstanding. Indeed, he reflected, with a certain wry amusement, if he had not been a King, he doubted that anyone would grant him so much as a second glance. But he had a loving heart — a loving and an *empty* heart, by God! And he was one who needed to give love as well as to receive it. Adore his three surviving bairns though he did, that was not enough to fill the emptiness. Mayhap this comely boy lying here might soothe the ache of a deprived heart.

Creeping to the door, King James resolved to call upon Robert Kerr every day until the laddie should be quite recovered.

★ ★ ★

Within the next few weeks, the Court and the superseded Earl of Montgomery were forced to accept the fact that the King had found another favourite. His Majesty was constantly at Sir Robert Rider's house with dainties for the invalid's physical well-being and Latin books for his mental edification. Young Kerr had no objection to the wine, jellies, sweet cakes and comfits, but his heart sank at the sight of the grammar-books, although he struggled manfully to learn, realising that his future might depend upon his mastery of the Latin tongue.

It was useless; he could not do it, but as events transpired, the King became so infatuated that in the end he forebore to insist upon the lessons. Robert discovered that his future was to depend upon a very different course of behaviour. The King was in love with him and expected consent, if not response. The matter required some consideration and Robert contemplated all the implications with due care.

It did not take him long.

After all, he reasoned, the matter would involve doing some violence to his natural inclinations, but would not the probable rewards far outweigh the inconvenience? Why, he might even get a knighthood and a place at Court! Certainly money and jewels would be forthcoming for comparatively little effort on his part, whereas no amount of Latin grammar could produce the same result, Latin being quite beyond his capabilities. Preferment from the King was a great chance to be offered at the age of twenty-one for no more than a fall from a horse! He would never get such another opportunity, so why be mealy-mouthed? Besides, His Majesty was a kind old gaffer and rarely generous, it seemed. Surely it would be easy enough to keep him kind, so long as he could stomach the constant kissing, fondling and probable bedding that his acceptance would entail. Och away, what of it? concluded Robert. Everything had its price and this should bring a goodly payment. So he would accept and pray that luck would be with him in it.

That was at the beginning of April. By December, he was Sir Robert Carr, a knight, a Gentleman of the Bedchamber, richly dressed and bejwelled and very pleased with himself.

He had decided to anglicise his name for, as he said to the lovesick King James: "Folk *will* call me Cur, as if I were a dog — mayhap they think it fits? Anyhap, I have changed the spelling in order that it may be pronounced correctly."

"Och, thou'rt a canny little darlin'," had crooned His Majesty, kissing Robert's cheek, "and as for being a dog, why, ye're ma own little lap-doggie, amn't ye? How I love ye, sweetheart! Ye luke sae braw in that bonnie white velvet suit that I'm fain tae gie ye a present."

"What, another present?" laughed Robert. "Ye snow me under with gifts!"

"And why not, then? Your old Dad and Gossip likes tae gie ye gifts. Here take this ring; 'tis a fine diamond and will set your hand off well." So saying, he pulled a large ring from his forefinger and pushed it upon Robert's own, his dark eyes soft with affection.

Ah, but he loved the dear laddie. Robbie was the sun in his heaven, the embodiment of his dreams. Nothing was or could be too good for the boy, for was he not incorruptible, immune to bribes? Eh, but he was a very Sir Galahad, the laddie. James gave a sigh of pure happiness as he recalled how dearest Robbie had come to him, all a-puzzle, to say that he had been offered a gift in order to influence His Majesty on a certain gentleman's behalf and what should he do about it?

"Do nothing, lovie," had advised the King. "What ye have done in telling me of it was the right thing."

"Well, I need no more money, nor jewels," Robert had said, smiling, "for do you not load me with such? I need no bribe to ask your help for someone. I would do it for nothing."

"Ay, and if I want tae help the gent who asked ye, I'll do it in ma own way and in ma own gude time. Ye're a dear, true-hearted laddie and I love ye for it, even though ye canna — "

" — speak Latin!" had finished Robert, grinning. "But I'm unco' good at the French, Sire, you must admit that."

The King laughed. "Na, na, darlin', Dr. de Mayerne says he canna understand a word ye say in the language! What d'ye say to that?" Seeing Robert's downcast look, he patted the young man's hand. "Ne'er mind, ma Robbie, I love ye for yourself, not for what ye can do. Come, 'tis a cold afternoon, the day. Let us pull up to the fire and play at dice, boysie.

Will ye humour your old Dad?"

So under the jealous eyes of the courtiers, a table was brought with a board and dice for the King and Sir Robert Carr to play backgammon.

3

ENTER MR. OVERBURY.

1609

ON a cold spring afternoon in 1609, Mr. Thomas Overbury, now twenty-six years old, disembarked from a ship moored in the Thames and made for the nearest tavern and hot spiced wine to take off the chill. He was newly returned from the Netherlands and, rather than ride from the coast in the biting wind, had boarded a small merchantman calling at Dover on the way to its destination in London. His mood was sour and depressed, for his travel abroad had not proved remunerative and no fat diplomatic post had fallen his way, despite his brilliant attainments, perhaps because of his bitterly sarcastic manner and undisguised conceit. He was also desperately short of money, as his threadbare cloak, shabby hat, worn brown doublet and scuffed leather boots testified all too plainly.

After fumbling in the sadly depleted purse at his belt and paying for his drink, he returned the landlord's friendly nod with a curt one of his own, his hands clasped round the steaming tankard for warmth.

"New to London?" enquired the landlord, interested in his customer's down-at-heel appearance which contrasted so strongly with his disdainful expression and the haughty carriage of his head.

"No," responded Mr. Overbury laconically, seeming more desirous of silence than speech.

"Been in foreign parts, then?" persisted the landlord.

"Ay," nodded Mr. Overbury.

"I'll warrant you're glad to be back," went on the publican. "No place like London, to my mind. You're short o' news, I wouldn't wonder. The King has his favourites and it seems that the latest has properly got his heart. He likes men better nor women, ye see. Wouldn't do for me, but there, it takes different fruits to make a pudden, don't it?"

Mr. Overbury permitted himself an indifferent shrug of the shoulders and applied himself to his wine. "It is of no interest to me," he said shortly. "The Court cares nothing for me, nor I for it."

"Why, hast been to Court?" The landlord stared incredulously at Mr. Overbury. "Excuse me, sir, but ye don't look as — "

" — as though I'm speaking the truth!" finished Mr. Overbury. "I've fallen on bad times through having no preferment from that Court, so now you know!" He buried his face in his tankard and took a long draught.

"I'm sorry to hear that, sir," said the inn-keeper. "Maybe if ye was to speak to the King's favourite, he'd put in a word for ye. 'Tis said as he's a right kind-hearted young gent and generous, too."

"Gossip will say anything," sneered Overbury. "I pay it no heed. Anyhap what is the name of this paragon of a King's pet who is reputed to be so large-hearted and who might put in a word for me?" His mouth twisted derisively.

"Oh, I can tell ye that!" The inn-keeper's round face creased in a smile, "'Tis Carr. Sir Robert Carr."

"*What!*" Mr. Overbury slammed down his tankard so hard that its contents slopped over the edge. "Robert Carr? I don't believe it! Is he a Scot? A red-haired Scot who has lived a while in France?"

"Well, I an't sure about him living in France, sir, but I do know as he's a Scot, ay, and that his hair be red. I seen him a-riding about the City with the King and he don't stint his gold, neither; throws plenty to the poor, he do." He stared curiously at Overbury whose glum expression had been replaced by one of excited urgency. "Do ye know him, sir?"

"By God!" Thomas Overbury gave a rather wild laugh. "If he is the one I think him to be, we were boys together! Mayhap my wretched luck has turned at last. *Sir* Robert Carr, you say? Oho, *that*'s new! I'd best go and try my fortune, eh landlord? If this Carr is my man, my troubles are over. Here — " with unaccustomed generosity he dived into his flat purse and brought out a coin, " — take this for your news. Now I have but one silver penny left and that shall hire a horse to take me to Whitehall Palace. Good day to ye, fellow, and my thanks!"

Catching up the bundle that contained his few possessions, Overbury strode out into the street, his head up, his step light, his heart full of hope.

* * *

Firelight flickered on warm panelled walls, on bright tapestries depicting classical scenes, on wooden chairs lustrous with polish and cushioned in purple, crimson and blue velvet. It caught reflections from the glass in the diamond paned windows and sparkled in the jewels on the yellow velvet doublet of a young man sitting close to the fire, for the afternoon was cold and the wind raw.

Sir Robert Carr was alone. His King and patron was attending a Council meeting and had invited Sir Robert to accompany him, but Robert had refused, saying that he had not enough knowledge of politics and did not enjoy appearing a dullard before the amused and disparaging eyes of the other Council members. He had no friends for, as the courtiers remarked, he would not take bribes, told the truth and was naive to a ridiculous degree. Indeed sniggered the courtiers, direly jealous, Sir Robert Carr appeared to possess the mind of a backward child in the body of a man.

The courtiers exaggerated, as was their spiteful wont. Robert Carr's mind, although guileless and rather uninformed, was not backward. Rather, it was not a courtier's mind, light and quick, eager for gossip and innuendo, ready with jest and wicked wit, but ponderous, slow to learn and equally slow to forget. Nor was his heart a courtier's heart, hard and cynical, but credulous and warm. He felt out of place and with reason. Therefore, he sat solitary, surrounded by the evidences of wealth and favour, feeling lonely and more than a little downcast at feeling so. It would have been fine, he thought, if Prince Henry, the King's eldest son, had not regarded him with such immovable dislike, and yet he could understand that. It could be no happy thing to see one's father caressing and petting a man — no indeed. Yet if the Prince had merely treated him with indifference, that would have been bearable; as matters stood, open loathing and outright insults were Robert's portion from Prince Henry. And because of this, few courtiers deigned so much as to exchange more than a curt sentence or two with Sir Robert Carr. It was a strange business. He wished he had someone to talk to and be merry with; it would make life less friendless.

When the door opened, he glanced up hopefully, but it revealed only a manservant bowing on the threshold.

"A gentleman to see you, Sir Robert," said the man respectfully.

"Oh ay, and what is his name? What does he want?"

"It is Tom, Robin," said a well-remembered voice from the door and Robert leaped to his feet with a cry of pleasure.

"Tom! Tom Overbury! Och, but I'm glad to see you, Tom! Come in, come in and warm yourself. Where have you been? What are you doing now? Do you stay in London?"

Relieved at the warmth of his welcome, Thomas, laughing, allowed himself to be led to a seat near the fire, where Robert, taking stock of his friend, was shocked at his shabby appearance.

"What am I doing now?" repeated Tom, the greetings over. "The answer is — nothing. I got no preferment at home and none abroad, so am returned penniless, wellnigh a beggar. Thus I am come to you, hoping for your help as a friend. And that is the bald truth."

"And you shall have my help!" cried Robert at once. "Why, 'tis a shame that such wit and learning as yours should go unpraised and unrecognised. Where do you lodge?"

"Nowhere," admitted Tom with a rueful grimace. "I have but just come from the boat. All I possess is in that bundle cast in the corner over there, whereas you — why, you are a very popinjay of finery, Robin."

"Well, you shall stay here," said Robert, clapping his friend on the shoulder, "and I shall speak to the

49

King about you tomorrow. I have a suite of several rooms here in the palace and you shall lodge in comfort." He gave an embarrassed grin. "As to my finery — ah — it pleases His Majesty to see me fine and — well — there you have it."

"Your elegance is not unearned, I take it? The King can scarcely be so altruistic, surely?" Tom's look was knowing and sly.

Robert's fair cheeks flushed a bright red. "No Tom, you are right. It is not unearned, I fear. His Majesty loves me as a man loves a — " He hesitated, at a loss for words.

"As a man loves a woman, I apprehend," said Thomas, who was seldom at a loss for words. "So. One must live, must one not?" He shrugged. "One must be a realist, after all. But I never thought of you as a realist, Rob, nor as one of the King's leanings and persuasion."

Robert flushed redder yet. "Oh, but I am not!" he exclaimed eagerly. "Not of the King's persuasion I mean."

"Then why — " Tom was puzzled until, a glass of wine in one hand and a piece of marchpane in the other, his feet upon a cushioned stool, he heard the full story of the accident and His Majesty's care and subsequent infatuation for young Robert Carr.

"And as to that, I suppose I must be a realist, in part," finished Robert, rather shamefaced, "or I would not have accepted the King's terms, would I?"

There was a silence as each marshalled his thoughts, Robert's confused, Tom's to a purpose.

"Would you accept my terms?" asked Overbury suddenly.

"Yours Tom? Why should there be terms between us? And anyhap, you rogue," Robert said, bursting into a laugh, "was it not you who was just now suing *me* for help? We need no 'terms' you and I. What one gives in friendship is free, Tom."

The tall rangy Overbury sent Robert a long look. Sweet Jesus, in spite of his intimacy with the King, the lad was as much an innocent as ever! And so very attractive; even more so than when they had first met in Scotland. Surely now that Robin had accepted King James's physical attentions he would not refuse

Tom's? Of the several men and women who had been his lovers, none had appealed to him as much as Robin Carr. He would chance it.

"I mean," he said slowly and deliberately, "if the King be your lover, will you not be mine? Is that direct enough for you?"

Robert started as though he had been shot. "Why, Tom! Is it — do you — are you — ? *Tom!*" He stared at Overbury, open-mouthed.

"Well, is it so strange?" said the other, brows raised. "'Tis a fashionable failing these days."

Robert swallowed hard. "Ay, but for me 'tis difficult enough to manage one such!" he blurted out uncomfortably. "It is unnatural to me, Tom. I do it for expedience only, you understand. It is no pleasure. Mind, His Majesty is a goodhearted old fellow, but he is a man, choose how, and I — well, I — " He stumbled to a stop.

"Oh, very well," said Overbury carelessly, not wishing to antagonise his friend. "Think no more of it, Robin. I am not so inflexible that I would refuse a woman, you know. It is just that I incline both ways. So I ask no more than that you might give me a place for old times sake. You will not be sorry, I promise you."

In the event, Robert was to be very sorry indeed, but that was in the future and as yet unrevealed.

★ ★ ★

Mr. Overbury got his place and, feeling greatly relieved, borrowed money from Robert in order to buy new clothes and make a presentable appearance at Court. He did not overspend, laying out enough gold for a cheap suit only and keeping the rest in his pocket, for who knew if his situation would prove secure? Life was a chancy thing. Consider the fortunes of Tom and Robert, for example. There was Robert, thick as a bolster, high in favour for playing naught but a few bed-games, and here was Thomas, possessing one of the best sets of brains in the land, nowhere at all. So, now that he had got a foothold, he must put those brains to work to make sure that he be not dislodged.

Rob was no man of letters, nor did he understand men and politics, for all that he held a position that, with a little help, could become uniquely powerful. Then Tom would provide that help so that he and Robin could scale the heights together. He resolved to make himself indispensable to Sir Robert Carr.

His opportunity came the very next day.

The two young men were sitting at ease, chatting in Robert's apartments, the King having retired for his usual afternoon nap. Tom set his wine-cup down on a nearby table and leaned forward in his chair, his face thoughtful.

"You say that you are admitted to His Majesty's Council, Robin. What do you have to say at these meetings?"

"Why, nothing at all, when I go," confessed Robert, somewhat abashed. "What can I say? I am ignorant of politics, so I do not attend many meetings for fear of being laughed at. The others think me a dullard. I know no Latin, I cannot discuss affairs of state. There was a Dutch business talked about the other day and a fine ninny I felt, sitting there mum as a stock."

"What was the business?" Tom, interested, lay back in his chair.

Robert frowned in an effort to remember. "Well, it seems that the King is right short of money, even though Lord Salisbury, as Lord Treasurer, has raised new taxes."

"Come, you are not so ignorant, then!" Tom was encouraging.

"Oh, I do but repeat what I heard," said Robert, "that is all."

"So what else did you hear? Tell me."

"I gather that the Dutch people owe the King some eight-hundred thousand pounds for help given by old Queen Elizabeth in the war with Spain and that he holds, as security, some Dutch towns."

Overbury nodded. "Ay, the towns of Flushing, Brill and Rammekens."

"Ah, you know of it, then! You see what an ignoramus I am, Tom."

"Nay, never mind. Go on."

"Well, the Dutch cannot pay, you see, and His Majesty must have the money.

He thinks he might sell the towns to the King of Spain."

Tom gave a crack of laughter. "Lord! What did the Councillors say to *that*?"

"They talked for hours, for and against," said Robert, "but found no answer."

"And what reason gave those who were against?"

"Oh, as far as I can remember, they said that such a sale would be seen as a betrayal of the Protestant cause and make for grave discontent in England. And there I sat, like a statue," he grumbled, reliving his grievance, "with nothing to say and no opinion to offer. They all think me a fool."

"Why should you have no opinion?" asked Tom.

"Because I do not understand the business."

"I'll wager," said Thomas, "that your fine Councillors understand the business no better than you, Rob. They conceal their ignorance better, that is all. Is the matter to be discussed again? It is? Now, listen to me. I have been in the Netherlands and have kept my ears open.

56

I do know of the business, so what I tell you will be true. Mark well what I say, remember it and convert it into your own words at the next Council meeting. You will find you need no Latin for that."

Robert seized his friend's hand in an impulsive grasp. "Oh Tom, I can see that you are to be my good angel! I will surely do as you say and will see what comes of it. How glad I am that you are back!"

And I shall make sure that you stay glad, thought Mr. Overbury, for it seems that I have fallen on my feet at last.

★ ★ ★

Sir Robert Carr took his place at the Council meeting that was held within the next few days. He had no proper seat, but sat upon a stool beside the King's great gilded armchair at the head of the long table, the King's arm about his shoulders, the King's hand toying with a lock of his hair. The debate rumbled on. No one could agree over what was to be done about the Dutch towns. The Earls of Northampton and Suffolk, being Catholic themselves, supported the sale of them to Catholic Spain, believing that this would assist friendly relations with that country. Robert Cecil, Earl of Salisbury and Lord Treasurer of the realm, opposed the move for the very good reason that the people of England would be violently against it.

It seemed that stalemate would again be reached and Robert, heart in mouth, made bold to speak.

"May I say a word, Your Majesty?"

The caressing hand dropped from Robert's hair and King James stared in amazement. "What, laddie? Nay, ye must not interfere — yet stay!" He gave a sudden chuckle. "Why not? None of us here can agree. Mayhap ye have a notion, eh?"

At this, the Councillors could scarcely restrain their merriment, struggling to contain themselves only out of respect for their royal master who was disposed thus to indulge his pet.

"Well, I have been considering this Dutch affair — " began Robert nervously. He got no further, for a burst of laughter, in which the King willingly joined, drowned his next words.

"Nay, let the laddie speak!" chortled His Majesty at last, wiping tears of mirth from his eyes. "And what is your opinion, then, Robbie?"

"Excuse my presumption, Your Majesty and my lords, but I have had an opportunity to learn somewhat of the matter from a gentleman newly returned from the Continent," said Robert as calmly as he could. "It appears that King Philip of Spain has no longer any interest in buying the towns."

"Has he not?" The King's grin had faded. "And why not, pray? Nay, cease your snickering ma lords! I wish tae hear Sir Robert's reply."

"The answer is that he cares not to waste money, Sire." Robert was gaining confidence. "If he wished to continue his war against the Netherlands, he would still desire the towns. But Spain's coffers are running low and I hear that within a few months she will be negotiating peace terms, so that if the towns are offered for sale now, the English will be furious, the Dutch resentful and the recovery of the debt more difficult than ever."

There was an astonished silence as the Lords of the Council stared at one another, open-mouthed at the emergence of such political acumen on the part of the favourite, hitherto regarded as nothing but a dressed-up empty-head.

"God's wounds!" exclaimed King James, thunderstruck. "And who is this gentleman tae whom ye have been talking, h'm?"

"It is a Mr. Overbury, Sire. I thought that, seeing Council had been discussing the Dutch question, I might assist their lordships by gathering information about this vexed matter." Robert had learned Mr. Overbury's lesson well and had spent many hours committing his words to memory.

"A Mr. Overbury, ye say? And who might he be that you or we should heed his words?" The King glanced about him, his face puzzled and enquiring.

Here Lord Salisbury raised a hand. "He is known to me, Sire," he said in his precise voice, "and a very shrewd and cautious young man he is — trustworthy, too. He has done me some service in the past. I think you may rely on his reports."

"Ay, Majesty," put in Robert eagerly, "for time will soon show if Mr. Overbury's reports be correct; a mere month or two, indeed. If the war should continue past that time, the sale can be considered again and we shall have lost nothing by waiting, while if peace be declared, why then, we can begin to press the Dutch for some restitution."

"Bless ma soul!" cried the King. "I must speak with this Mr. Overbury. It seems that he has a grasp of the subject, as even have you, ma dearest. Why, ye have been a verra Daniel of wisdom this day!" He patted Robert's cheek affectionately.

King James lost no time in seeking out Mr. Overbury. In response to his monarch's questions, Mr. Overbury expressed himself, wittily and well, going so far as to cap the King's Latin tags with some of his own.

"Ha, verra neat, by ma troth!" cried the King. "That is good, Mr. Overbury. Ye have a quick mind and know how tae use it, while your Latin is quite passable — for an Englishman."

Mr. Overbury bowed, hiding a grin.

"I am happy to assist you in any way possible, Sire."

"By God's feet!" exclaimed His Majesty, favouring Thomas with a closer look. "But I do remember ye! Ay, Lord Salisbury said ye had done him some service — ay, I remember the occasion now. Ye're the one wi' the woundy bitter tongue, as I recall. Best keep it bridled when I am by, ma lad, and dinna forget it." He frowned, studying the young man. "Have ye no' a better suit o' clothes than that ye wear, Mr. Overbury? D'ye need money, mon?"

Mindful of the gold he had received from Robert, most of which still lay in his purse and deciding that a little more would not come amiss, Mr. Overbury bowed again. "Your Majesty is most kind."

"Take this then," a heavy purse changed hands, "and smarten yourself up. For masel'," said the King, "I dinna gae fidget ma own person too much about dress, but I do like those about me tae present a stylish appearance, so make yourself spruce before we meet again."

So Thomas Overbury settled in at

Whitehall, soon to have rooms and servants of his own. Life promised a pleasant future, with pickings a-plenty. Thanks to Robert's good offices with King James, he was knighted in the June of that year and felt that his foot was firmly placed on the ladder of success at last. He was not popular; his biting tongue and intellectual arrogance made certain of that, but Robert needed him and, if Sir Thomas Overbury knew it, was going to need him for evermore.

His plans worked so well that all the Court were astounded at Sir Robert Carr's hitherto unsuspected gifts of statecraft, gifts which amounted to political genius for affairs both at home and abroad. The King was enchanted, while the wealthy and powerful Catholic Howard family began to regard the once-despised favourite as a force to be reckoned with, courting him with presents and flattery. Delighted at first, puzzled later, he consulted Overbury about this sudden access of friendship from those who had previously treated him with contempt.

"Oho!" nodded Thomas wisely. "I was waiting for this. Now hearken to me, Rob, and mind what I say. Hold back from the Howards, for the more you withdraw, the more they will court you. And, because the King holds them in high esteem, the more they pursue you, the more His Majesty will favour you." *And work to my own advantage*, he added inwardly.

For His Majesty did not favour Tom Overbury and Tom Overbury knew it. The King was jealous of Tom's friendship with his adored Robbie, irritated by his undoubted scholarship and further annoyed by a witty little book Thomas had written, but just now published by Lisle, the bookseller, of St. Paul's Churchyard. His Majesty was deservedly proud of his own intellectual attainments and brooked no rival. However, not wishing to upset his Robbie by seeming to despise Overbury, he swallowed his chagrin, managing to dissemble his feelings of resentment and dislike enough to congratulate Sir Thomas, though rather curtly, upon his literary success. It did nothing to warm his heart to the young man.

Meanwhile, Henry Howard, Earl of Northampton, head of the house of Howard and his nephew Thomas Howard, Earl of Suffolk and Chamberlain of the Royal Household, had laid their heads together on the subject of Sir Robert Carr.

"If we can get his goodwill," said Lord Suffolk, rubbing his chin thoughtfully, "then we can rule the King."

"Of course," replied Northampton. "And once we have accomplished that, who knows what we might gain? Why, we might find it possible to strike a blow for the True Faith!" He paused, frowning. "What bait can we use to bring Carr within our net?"

Their Lordships were pacing up and down the pleached alley in the garden of Northampton House in the village of Charing Cross. It was a summer morning and the late May sun shone warmly down from a cloudless sky. Old Lord Northampton walked with a deliberate step, leaning upon his nephew's arm, his other hand clutching a gold-topped stick, his head, under a black velvet hat feathered with blue, poked forward like some eager bird of prey. Lord Suffolk, his dark brows creased in thought, marched steadily, supporting the weight of his elderly kinsman upon his arm.

"It would needs be a sweet bait," said Lord Suffolk.

Lord Northampton's bad leg had begun to ache. He halted. "Let us sit," he grunted, "upon that bank yonder. Come nephew, let us leave the alley to its shadows and rest ourselves out in the sun."

His nephew, assenting, led the way to a seat cut in a daisy-strewn grassy bank and assisted his relative to sit. At last this was achieved, though with much sighing and groaning, and once fairly settled, Lord Northampton spoke again.

"Would your daughter be sweet enough?" he asked.

Lord Suffolk started. "My daughter? Which daughter mean you, uncle — Elizabeth or Frances?"

"Use your wits!" barked Northampton impatiently, twisting his wrinkled face into a myriad cross-grained creases.

"Why, Frances of course. At present she has no husband to restrain her, yet being married, has more freedom than a maid."

"Well, but her husband may return at any time, uncle. He has been abroad for three years now and soon will be old enough to come home and claim her."

"So we shall have to work swift then," said Lord Northampton. "He will be eighteen next year, I believe, and will return then, I make no doubt. She is sixteen, is she not?"

"Sixteen this year, sir."

"She must be at Court more often, nephew. Put her in Carr's way and we shall see what transpires. I have noted that young Prince Henry has eyed her with interest when she had been present there, and other gentlemen too have appeared to look upon her with favour. She is a winsome lass."

"But what will His Majesty say? 'Twas he who arranged the match 'twixt her and Lord Essex, and she is virgin, remember."

"Good God, I do not mean that she is to sleep with Carr, merely to lead him on, entice him, fascinate him and bring him over to us!"

"But is Carr interested in women uncle? Would he even notice overtures from Frances?"

"As to that, we shall find out. Now give me my stick. I swear this grass is damp, plague take it! As I do not wish to spend the summer crippled with rheumatism, help me to my feet and quickly!" He snapped out his commands and his nephew hastened to obey.

"Will you speak to her, uncle, or shall I?"

"Oh, leave it to me. I'll deal with her. Let us walk down to the river and then go withindoors. Where is your arm? Come along, come along!"

Slowly they made their way along the gravelled walk to the water-gate, beyond which the river Thames slipped by, ripples gleaming glassy in the sunshine, both talking busily and discussing their plans.

4

FALES AND DANGEROUS DECEITS.

1609 – 1610

LORD NORTHAMPTON spoke to his great-niece of the project he had in mind and she did not seem averse to it. He was a little surprised, for he had expected virginal flutterings, if not outright refusal. The girl had known no man carnally, he was well aware, since her husband had never warmed her bed, being considered too young at the time of the marriage, besides which she had been kept very close and knew little of the world and its ways.

The sixteen year old Frances, Countess of Essex, was not averse to her uncle's plan because her fancy had been caught by Robert Carr from the moment he had galloped into the lists at the tourney on King's Day, three years before, but she had kept this to herself. Upon her very few visits to Court, she had watched him with eyes that had been at first worshipping, then desirous. She had wished most heartily that she could have been wedded to him, instead of to a boy but one year older than herself and one whom she hardly knew. Now her great-uncle was telling her that she was to spend more time at Court and to do her utmost to attract Carr to her side! She gazed dreamily out of the window, three of its panes open to catch the soft breeze wafting across the garden from the river, and smiled to herself.

"Remember," warned Northampton, "you need do no more than smile upon the fellow, flatter him and appear to be interested in him. Young and virgin as you are, I would not ask you to behave so at all, but in this case, the end justifies the means. It is for Our Family, you understand. Remember also that you must keep yourself for your husband — not that I imagine you will have much trouble in controlling the impulses of the King's precious fancy-man. However, you must try what you can do."

Receiving no immediate answer, he

grew impatient. "Well, child, well?" he barked. "I do not invite you and your parents to Northampton House for you to go into a trance when a scheme is put to you! Are you willing? Yes, or no?"

"Oh, I am willing, my lord uncle," she answered in a sweet languid voice. "I will do my best, but I think that Prince Henry may not like it, for I believe he favours me a little and he dislikes Robert Carr very greatly."

"The Prince? He will be too taken up with the preparations for the ceremony that is to create him Prince of Wales in a week or two to give an eye to what you do, take my word for it." Northampton glanced approvingly at the young girl disposed so gracefully upon the red velvet cushion of the window-seat, her white satin gown falling in elegant folds about her. She really was a pretty piece, he thought; her skin so white, her eyes so large and of such a clear light grey, her golden hair clustering in honey-gold curls about her forehead and small jewelled ears.

He gave a thoughtful grunt. Prince Henry, the King's elder son, soon to be

Prince of Wales, had certainly cast an eye in Frances's direction. Others had noticed it, too, and had murmured of it. Perhaps he had made a mistake in allowing his favourite niece to wed the Earl of Essex at the King's behest. Might it not have been better to have waited and set out lures for the Prince? What a prize would he have been for the Catholic Faith! Sure, the Prince was a stout Protestant, but he was young and marriageable and desire can work wonders with previously rigid-held notions — Northampton had noticed it often enough. He shrugged. Heigh-ho, what was done was done. 'Twas the present one must consider and to that object he would work.

"We join your cousin of Arundel and the Court at Richmond tomorrow," he said, "and you may begin to work your wiles at once, my girl."

Frances turned her head from the prospect at the window and gave him a dazzling smile. "Ay," approved her elderly kinsman, "smile at Carr like that and he will be at your feet, no matter what his tastes are, King's pet or no."

"Oh, he likes ladies," she told Lord

Northampton. "I saw him kiss Lady Trenchard behind a pillar once, when the King was not by."

"Well, your task will be all the easier then," remarked his lordship. "You had best go now and begin to make ready to leave for Richmond on the morrow. Go along now and remember to tell your maids to pack all your finest gowns. Once you are fairly settled at Court, your parents will go home, so mind you do as I bid you and mind you behave yourself in a seemly fashion at all times."

★ ★ ★

The weather was fine at Richmond, it was bright June and King James had arranged to go hunting. He felt lonely and a little depressed for Prince Henry's ceremonies were all done, the feasting was over and his son, instead of showing filial gratitude and affection, seemed more disapproving than ever. It was a sad thing, thought His Majesty, that a son should disapprove of his father and show it so openly, especially when that father would do almost anything

73

to please his son — anything but give up dearest Robbie, of course. And that was the root of the trouble. Henry hated the notion that his father could make favourites of men and made no secret of his feelings. But he did not understand, gloomed King James. He did not understand that his father could not help his tastes, that he loved Robbie, but that he also loved his dear son just as much, though in a different way.

Life could be very difficult, pondered James with a sigh. And moreover, gifted and learned though he was, he was not loved as universally as he would wish to be as a ruler. He longed to be loved; ached and yearned for it. Ay, it was the cross he was fated to carry through life, he realised, and he had gone to strange shifts at times, to ease the longing in his breast. Of course, being a King and thus divinely chosen, he could do no wrong, which was fortunate, for in this way he had nothing with which to reproach himself, although some folk did not seem to agree with him these days. Indeed, thought James, there were those in Parliament who had dared to criticise his spending, as if it were a crime to possess a generous nature!

Why, he had done his best to draw in funds! Had he not had the clever idea of selling honours? A gentleman could now become a baronet — a new name for a newly-devised title — for the sum of one thousand pounds paid to the Crown. Was not that a good notion? And many had availed themselves of it, had they not? And then he had enlarged the scheme to include other patents of nobility on a rising scale of fees, culminating in the payment of ten thousand pounds for an earldom which many had been glad enough to hand over their gold to obtain, thus serving to line His Majesty's pockets and the coffers of the Treasury. Lord Salisbury, the Lord Treasurer, who could have thought of it himself, should have been grateful to his sovereign rather than forever moaning of insolvency and debt.

Nor was James at all sure that he agreed with Lord Salisbury's latest notion for making money, a notion by which he, the King, would receive a yearly income guaranteed by Parliament, on the understanding that he would sacrifice the Crown's surviving feudal rights. It seemed to James that this would give too much power to Parliament while decreasing his own. Even now, discussions were in train, and not too happily, the members of Parliament being doubtful of releasing large sums into the hands of their King. Such insolence! It was scarcely to be borne. Why should he not give handsome presents to those he loved, pray? How dared those he loved be termed 'undeserving', or worse, 'Scottish', as though to be Scottish was shameful! Let them remember that their King was a Scot and proud to be, fumed James. Well, nothing would make him give up his darling Robbie, no matter what, and let them learn it!

As well as this, there were even some murmurs heard against his imprisonment of his cousin, the Lady Arabella Stuart. He had loved Arbell, ay, had loved her as a sweet pretty sister. He had assured her that he would be well content if she should choose a husband loyal to the Crown, so long as she would not make a foreign marriage without his consent — and what had she done? She had elected to fall in ·love with the one man in England who was totally unsuitable and whom James had completely overlooked, William Seymour, grandson of Lady Catherine Grey who had, in her lifetime, had a good claim to the throne! Since Arbell herself had an even closer claim, any children of such a union could pose a considerable threat to the Succession. James had therefore clapped the Lady Arabella and her William swiftly into the Tower, there to meditate upon their folly while he considered the matter. Why should anyone criticise him for this? It was only reasonable that he should treat such a grave matter with the seriousness it demanded. One could not afford to be sentimental over it and he meant Arbell no harm, merely for her to cool her hot blood.

Oh lackaday, what uneasy thoughts were these! Where was Robbie? He must have Robbie here, now, to comfort him, to drive dull care away and to ease the pain of the void within him.

And Robert came to his summons, to

hear confidences, to raise depression, to be fondled, kissed and petted — and to tell His Majesty that the hunt awaited his pleasure.

"Prince Henry is there too, Sire, with Prince Charles and the Queen. See, I am clad all in Lincoln green, a very huntsman, am I not? Will you not put on your hat and sling your hunting-horn on your belt? Come, think no more on worrisome things! The day is fair and we all long for your gracious presence."

The King caught at Robert's hand. "Is that true, darlin'? Do ye long for me?"

Robert drew a breath, then, seeing the real anguish in the dark eyes staring so appealingly into his own, gave a sweet reassuring smile and patted the King's shoulder. "You know that," he said. "Come, here's your hat. I'll put it on ye with such a saucy cock to it that ye'll outshine us all." And so saying, he placed the red-feathered green felt hat on King James's greying auburn head, pulling it jauntily to one side.

At once the King threw his arms round the young man, kissing his cheeks with protestations of eternal love and it was with difficulty that he could be persuaded to join the hunt at all. Once outside, Robert was only too aware of the glares sent him by Queen Anne and the Prince of Wales but, taking his place at the King's side, he did his best to remain courteous and in seeming ignorance of their overt animosity.

The stag was caught on a curve of the river bank opposite the village of Teddington and the party began to straggle homeward, King James riding this time with his family while Robert was left to choose his own company. He felt a need to be alone and was startled out of his thoughts by the sound of a woman's voice addressing him.

"I crave your pardon, Sir Robert, but I have dropped my glove somewhere about and I cannot see it. Could you, perhaps, help me to find it?"

Glancing up, he beheld the Countess of Essex mounted on a pretty grey mare. She was gazing at him, a look of hopeful entreaty upon her charming countenance. "Why, certainly, Lady Essex," he answered at once. "Your glove, did you say?"

"Yes, and it is a new one," she said.

"But just given to me by my uncle. It is of green leather, all silk stitched and pearl embroidered — very pretty and I should not like to lose it."

"Let us retrace our way a little," he suggested, watching as she turned her mount, grace and expertise in every movement. By the stars, but she was a lovely creature! Her curls, her small pert hat, her dashing gown, so low-cut as to show almost the whole of her delicate white breasts, ay indeed her husband was a lucky man, thought Robert Carr enviously. Yet her husband was away and she was a virgin wife, he believed. He would he were in Lord Essex's shoes to return home to claim such untried beauty instead of being yoked to an old — ! He pushed the thought back. Nay, he must not antagonise the source of all his good fortune.

Suddenly Lady Essex gave a cry. "Oh see, there it is!" Her surprise was well simulated. "Under that bush, look there!" She began to dismount, but he was before her, leaping to the ground in one agile movement to retrieve the glove.

When he turned, she was standing

behind him and he almost collided with her, being forced to seize her to save her from falling. She blushed, and it was the sweetest rosy pink. He thought he had never seen anything so enchanting and he could not at first loose her, experiencing the strongest desire to catch her to him and cover that flower face with kisses. Madness! He must keep his head. Would not His Majesty be enraged, not to mention the lady's powerful family who, no doubt, were keeping her for her husband?

"Here is your glove my Lady," he said, having difficulty in commanding his breathing. "Let me help you to re-mount."

They rode back through the fields to Richmond Palace, saying little but looking and thinking the more, their hearts beating fast beneath their elaborate silks and satins.

The first move in the Howard game had been played. The rest followed effortlessly, for Sir Robert Carr fell fathoms deep in love.

"Tom, I adore her," he told his friend as they rode in the park at Windsor one fine September day. "She fills my mind so that I can think of nothing else. She fills my dreams, Tom."

"Why, what do you hope to gain?" sniffed Overbury scornfully. "Her husband will come home and that will be that."

"I cannot endure the thought!" cried Robert, desperation in his tone. "I would be with her day and night. Oh, if only this could be! I doubt she understands how I feel."

"Write to her then," advised Thomas, bored by these raptures, "and tell her. It should serve to flatter her considerable vanity."

"Oh, you are severe! She is not vain, merely sweetly young and sprightly, the pretty angel."

"She is a Howard and I have no time for any of that crew," replied Thomas shortly. "They treat me as though I do not exist, so you cannot expect me to feel friendly toward any one of them. I deem them self-seeking and arrogant and if the old ones are, so will the young ones be. They will use you so long as it suits them, Robin, then drop you like a hot coal if aught go amiss."

Robert laughed. "Why, what should go amiss? How you prate, Tom!" He paused, struck by a sudden thought. "You say to write to Frances, but what sort of a letter would I be able to scrawl? I cannot put words together, you know that well. And as for words of love — impossible!" He glanced at Overbury whose face expressed nothing but weary disinterest.

They rode under the great trees in silence, each occupied by his own cares and concerns, until Robert spoke again. "Tom," he said tentatively, "would you write to her for me?"

Overbury, taken by surprise, jerked the rein, so that his mount pranced and curvetted. "*What!* You jest!"

"Nay, I do not. I'll make it worth your while, Tom."

There was another silence.

"Very well," said Overbury, after some consideration, "I'll do it." He burst into a loud laugh. "By God, what a joke! It truly is a joke, Rob. When I think of that haughty piece sighing over my passionate words, thinking they come from you, I cannot help but laugh."

Robert did not share his friend's amusement. "You do not like her, Tom. Why not?"

Overbury's smile faded. "Ah, how can I tell?" he countered irritably. "Once a Howard, always a Howard, that is all. We all have our fancies and she is not mine. I cannot be your mirror in everything, Rob."

"No, no, of course not." Robert was all swift compunction. "Perhaps I am unfair to you, Tom. But I confess freely that I could not go on without you. I know that you are not appreciated as you deserve, but I am not one of your detractors, so do not snap at me. I am your friend and wish you only well."

"Ay, I realise that. You are nothing without me and I, curse it, am nothing without you!" Thomas jerked his horse's reins again, causing the animal to dance restlessly.

"It chafes you, does it not?" observed Robert sympathetically. "I can well understand it. For you, with your brains, to be dependent on a dullard like me must be very galling."

"You are too kind-hearted for your

own good," replied Overbury, touched by this ingenuous tribute. "It will pay you no wages in the end, you know. I will write your plaguey letters, Robin, and I promise you that they will be lyrical and loving enough to melt the hardest heart."

"You will read me what you write?"

"Of course. You must be able to quote your supposed effusions, must you not? Leave it to me. Come, heels in — I'll race you — come!" And away he galloped, the hooves of his bay flying, Robert on his big chestnut following speedily behind.

★ ★ ★

For herself, Frances, Countess of Essex, was wildly in love with the King's handsome red-haired favourite and was by no means sure that her feelings were returned, losing much sleep in her agitation over this. She had few friends at Court, having come there so recently and also because the interest her presence had caused among the men had aroused a certain amount of jealousy among the ladies. So, lacking a confidante, she turned to a pretty, blonde, fashionable woman who, in Frances's childhood had acted as her part-servant and part-companion, a Mrs. Anne Turner.

Mrs. Anne was not an entirely suitable choice as a friend for an impressionable sixteen year old suffering from the pangs of first love, for she dealt in drugs to stimulate backward lovers, potions to depress the ardours of the over-eager, while allowing her house to be used for secret assignations. Her elderly husband, being ill and confined to his room, knew nothing of her activities which paid her very well. Further supplies of remedies she obtained from a certain Dr. Simon Forman, a learned and clever practitioner and astrologer, who had extensive knowledge of herbs and drugs. Not content with her thriving business, Mrs. Turner had also invented a special starch which, being yellow and therefore different from any starch yet seen, found instant favour with the lords and ladies of the Court; yellow becoming the only colour admissible for the lace collars and cuffs then in vogue. The lady was thus looked upon with approbation and treated with great circumspection by those who paid for her services.

Noticing the dark shadows under Frances's eyes and her unusual pallor, Mrs. Turner ventured to enquire the reason.

"What is it, Lady Frances, my dear?" she asked in her peculiarly sweet and ingratiating fashion. "You look sad, which is strange in one so beautiful and highly-placed."

Frances threw down the embroidery upon which she had been engaged, tossing her head pettishly. "Well, I am sad," she agreed, her voice a childish whine. "What is there to make me happy? No one likes me here, for one thing, and for another, my wretched husband will be home soon. Is that not enough?"

"Hush, hush," warned Mrs. Anne, seeing the heads of other ladies in the withdrawing chamber begin to turn. "You do not want the whole Court to learn your feelings do you, my Lady? Besides, your husband may have grown into a very proper man by now. He is rich, he has a great estate and has the King's favour. You might be very pleased with him."

"That is all you know!" snapped Frances under her breath and near a sob. Biting her lips, she jumped to her feet and flounced to a window, staring out unseeingly over the gardens of Whitehall where a few late roses still bloomed in the parterres. Hastily, Mrs. Anne rose and followed her.

"Come, come, my Lady, do not give way here," she urged. "There is a small ante-chamber nearby where we may be private and you may tell me what is in your mind." She took Frances by the arm and led her out of the room to escape the gaze of eyes already growing curious and lips beginning to whisper inquisitively.

Once in the ante-chamber, Frances flung herself into a chair as Mrs. Anne closed the doors, making sure that no eavesdroppers were within earshot.

"I wish my husband would die abroad!" burst out the young girl, twisting her hands convulsively. "I shall not welcome him home, depend on it!"

"Dear me," observed Mrs. Turner, her

blue eyes sparkling with interest, "what ails my Lady?"

"I am in love, that is what ails me!" cried Frances. "And I know not if he loves me in return. It is driving me half-witted!"

"Ah, I understand." Mrs. Turner's voice was soothing, inviting confidences. "And who is the gentleman, dearest?"

"It is Sir Robert Carr," confessed Frances, her mouth trembling. "He stares at me and often seems wishful to speak, but says and does naught. I thought that he did like ladies, but there are so many who say he beds only with men. In which case what hope is there for me?"

Anne Turner's tongue darted out and licked her lips. What a delicious piece of scandal was this and how profitable it promised to be if managed well!

"Oh, there is plenty of hope for you, my Lady," she smiled. "I agree with you and do not believe Sir Robert to be an arsy-varsy, for all that the King is in love with him. I have seen him eye the ladies right lecherously, even kissing a maidservant or two when he imagined no one was by. I keep my eyes open, you see. And if he do be a backside-forward, why, I have certain nostrums to produce a masculine response when necessary."

Frances clasped her hands, her face alight. "*You* have, Anne? You have potions to produce love? Oh, you must help me and at once. I will pay you well," she added.

"In that case," answered Mrs. Anne with bright satisfaction, "your troubles are over, my Lady. I will bring a powerful love-potion to you tomorrow."

"But how can I make him take it?" asked Frances. "What must I do?"

Mrs. Anne almost laughed at the girl's artlessness. "You must pour what I give you into a goblet of wine and hand it to him with your sweetest smile," she advised, "and I promise you that results will not be long forthcoming. But remember, this must be a secret between you and me. You must tell no one."

Frances hesitated. "Is the potion dangerous, Anne? It will not harm him, will it? Perhaps I had better not — " She paused uncertainly.

"Oh, it is quite harmless," Mrs. Turner answered reassuringly. "Many have taken it with excellent effects. Besides, it is a means to an end, is it not?"

"Why, that is something like the words my uncle often uses!" exclaimed Frances, impressed. "He says that the end justifies the means."

"And he is quite right," agreed Mrs. Anne firmly. She smiled. "Fear not my Lady, all will be as you desire. I will help you in any way you wish. I am yours to command."

Jumping to her feet, Frances flung her arms round Mrs. Turner's neck. "Oh Anne, dear Anne!" she cried. "If you do this for me I will give you my pearl necklace as well as your fee. How glad I am that you are here with me!"

And how glad am I, thought Mrs. Turner, *for you will add to my funds, Lady Essex.*

It was by an odd quirk of coincidence that on the night before Lady Frances decided to slip a love-philtre into Sir Robert Carr's wine-cup, Thomas Overbury had penned the last words of an ardent love-letter, signed by Robert, to be given to her in secret the next day.

On that day, she contrived to place

herself near to the favourite in the Long Gallery at Whitehall, where many of the courtiers had congregated after playing at battledore and shuttlecock in the orchard. Greeting him with becoming modesty, she offered to pour him a measure of wine. The ready flush mounted to his cheeks as, taken by surprise, he bowed in response.

"Nay, my Lady," he protested, "surely 'tis I who should be doing this for you, rather than you should act the servant for me."

"It is my pleasure, Sir Robert," she replied, shyly but firmly. "You played right hard outside and now must be over-warm." She gestured to the windows. "See how the sun shines on the river, although it be late September, and look at the boats upon the water! Do you not wish you were in a boat, enjoying the river breezes?"

Following the direction of her pointing hand, he turned and looked through the leaded panes at the lively scene below. Several small decorated boats containing gaily dressed citizens and musicians had gathered and were being rowed upstream, clearly bent on a party of pleasure. Noting their air of jolly freedom, the restrictions of his position overcame him for a moment, but for a moment only, and he turned back to Frances once more, but not before she had gained time to slip the potion, unseen by anyone, into his goblet.

"Will it please you to walk in the gallery with me, Lady Essex?" he asked her, raising the jewel-studded cup to his lips. "I would take it as a great honour."

"But shall we not be marked and observed?" she queried. "Will not this cause gossip?"

He gave a rueful laugh. "What of it? Most folk here think me to have no interest in women, so they will make little of it. Your reputation is safe enough with me, I fear."

She smiled and began to pace slowly up the long room at his side, her heart beating fast with shyness and yearning, chattering aimlessly of this and that, while inwardly wondering if Mrs. Turner's potion would have an effect and, if so, what form it would take.

The object of her interest contributed little to the conversation, struggling as he was to overcome an almost overwhelming rush of desire caused by the working of the drug, together with his own natural feelings. This surge of lust was so strong that it became all he could do to restrain himself from tearing Lady Essex's clothes from her body and leaping upon her then and there. The physical manifestation of this urge suddenly grew so uncomfortably obvious that in sheer embarrassment and dismay he mumbled a few words, pushed a note into her hand and fairly ran out of the gallery, leaving Frances bewildered, the note crushed in her hand.

"What, Lady Frances!" cried a wag, bursting with laughter. "Has the King's sweetheart taken fright at your feminine charms? Sure, the pretty fellow is at a loss with the ladies, especially one so winsome as yourself!"

Fighting for composure, Frances managed to make a smiling rejoinder before finding a secluded alcove where it might be possible to read her note. She deciphered only a few lines, then folded it quickly and thrust it into her bodice.

What a letter! She wondered that the fire it contained had not caused the paper to burn up of itself! Surely Mrs. Turner's potion must have worked right fast, but when did he write the note? She drew an ecstatic breath. Oh, he must really love her, then, for he had written the note before they had met in the gallery! Sexually innocent as she was, she was puzzled that he should leave her with such graceless haste. Perhaps he longed to kiss her? Oh, she did not know, but she must be alone to read the rest of the note and to give rein to her feelings of joy and exhilaration. Swiftly she sought out her cousin, Lord Arundel, who was playing at ninepins at the far end of the gallery.

"Cousin," she said softly, "I am sorry to interrupt your game, but I have the migraine very badly and must go to my room. Will you please make my apologies to His Majesty when he comes?"

"Ay, you do look right pasty, Frank," responded her cousin bluntly, glancing up. "Best you should rest abed with the curtains drawn. I'll make your excuses, never fear. Get along with you now, 'tis

95

my turn to aim. Set up the pins, Jack, 'tis my throw. Come, make ready man!"

Behind the curtains of her bed in the little slip of a chamber she was fortunate to have to herself in the crowded palace of two thousand rooms, Frances read her letter to the end. It was beautiful, burning with poetry and passion, and he wrote that he loved her to distraction. She rolled over, burying her face in the pillow, shuddering with excitement and delight. They must meet, they must be alone! Oh, what if his ardour should cool if it were too difficult for them to be often alone? She must speak to Mrs. Anne. Mrs. Anne would help her. Frances felt herself to be the happiest, luckiest girl in the world. How perfect it was to be Frances Howard! She drew in her breath with a sudden hiss.

She was not Frances Howard.

No, and never again so to be. She was now Frances Devereux, Countess of Essex, wife to a man she had seen only on her marriage day three years ago. A man? Her husband was but a lad of seventeen years old at this time. What did she want with a boy one year older than herself when the wonderful and radiant Robert Carr, seven years her senior, high in favour and the handsomest man at Court, professed himself to be nigh dead for love of her? Her head spun with the thrill of it, her legs felt weak and her stomach seemed to have turned to water at the mere thought of the bliss that would be hers with the beautiful Robert Carr, if only — ! Oh, if only she were not wed! Jesus, what should she do when Essex came home to claim her?

She clenched her little fists. If she, Frances, had anything to do with it, Robert Carr should have her first. Robert Carr *must* have her first! They would contrive it somehow. There must be a way, there had to be, or the Lord only knew what she would do. Something desperate, anyhap, she told herself, tossing restlessly from side to side, fretting herself into a headache in reality.

Ringing the handbell for her maid-servant, she sent the woman scurrying for Mrs. Anne Turner. "Fetch her to me at once, Dorothy, for I die of the headache. Go quick, Doll — hurry!"

When Mrs. Turner arrived at Frances's bedside, all in a rush, a remedy in a glass held in her hand, the Countess, now quite flushed and feverish, greeted her with a cry of relief. "Oh Anne, Anne! What am I to do? Oh, very well, I will drink your medicine, but you must help me. Your potion worked with Sir Robert; he loves me, Anne! He says he is desperate for love of me and longs to make me his own. See, here is his letter."

"You wish me to read it, my Lady?" Mrs. Turner's blue eyes grew sharp with eagerness. Did not my Lady realise that she was putting herself in Mrs. Anne's power by her ingenuous confidences? Mrs. Anne was not one to let slip such an opportunity. Setting the empty glass down upon a chest-top she stretched out a hand for the letter which Frances willingly gave her.

"Lord save us!" she giggled when she had read it. "Who would have thought it? He is afire, poor gentleman, and he is the King's lover, also! He is a man of talent, surely!"

"Your potion is of great power," said

Frances. "How did you prepare it?"

"Nay, it is not one of mine," said Mrs. Turner. "I had this from Dr. Simon Forman of Lambeth who is marvellous learned in medicines. I paid him well for it, too," she added meaningly.

"Oh, I will repay you!" cried Frances at once. "Tell me the price and I will give you the money now. Ay, and you must take the necklace I promised you; it is in the drawer of that chest. Do get it, Anne. Yes, it suits you very well. Now, can you get more of this philtre from Dr. Forman, think you?"

"Why, certainly," answered Mrs. Anne, gazing admiringly at herself and the necklace in the Countess's silver hand-mirror. "But it is very expensive and to get it I must pay a waterman for a boat across to Lambeth and back. You see, my Lady, my poor old husband is unwell, medicines are not cheap and there are my children eating their heads off. It is not easy for me to contrive with so many cares hanging about me." All very commendable and pathetic, but she did not see fit to mention that her lover, Sir Arthur Mainwaring, kept her well supplied with money and gifts. Why spoil a good source of revenue? Mrs. Anne was no philanthropist.

"See, I have gold with me," said Frances, placing several gold pieces into Mrs. Turner's ready palm. "Is that enough for another philtre? I do not wish Sir Robert's love to fade before we can meet again."

"If he is as hot as his letter," smirked Mrs. Anne, "I should judge there is no danger of that, but I will get the potion for you, my Lady. 'Twill do no harm to have it by you."

To Frances's ecstatic happiness, letter followed letter, each more lyrical and fervent than the last, Sir Thomas Overbury gaining a certain perverted pleasure and cynical amusement from their composition. Robert's gratitude was unbounded and so were the gifts he lavished upon his friend who was never heard to refuse the largesse heaped upon him, regarding it only as his due.

Frances and Robert met whenever it was possible for them to do so, passing from words to kisses, from kisses to love-play and from love-play to consummation in a very short time. They talked often, and with anguish, of the return of Lord Essex.

"He is due to show his face at any time now," she said wildly, one cold day in November, when she and Robert were curled up naked in Robert's bed, the King having retired for his customary afternoon nap. "You realise, do you not, that he will expect to bed me? I tell you, I will not, *will not* sleep with him! I will not, Robbie!" She began to sob and throw herself about in the bed. "How can I take him after you? I love you and I want no one else!"

He tried to soothe her. "Hush darling, do not agitate yourself. There must be something that we can do."

"Well, what then? Tell me what? I can see no way out for us. He will come and claim me and take me away to Chartley and we might never meet again. What say you to that?"

"Oh God!" Robert groaned aloud. "We must be together. We must meet! I cannot live without you. What is more, I cannot endure the thought of you lying abed with him, of him treating you as a wife, making free with your body. Your lovely body which is mine, Frances, mine! Oh God it is too unbearable to contemplate!"

She set her pretty chin. "Well, I will promise you one thing. He will never make free with my body — never while I live. I swear it. I swear it on the sacred blood of Jesus!" she cried, her eyes flashing. "Ah, you do not believe me, I can tell that by your face, but you will find out, Robbie. I will have my way. I always have my way — you will see!"

"But your parents!" he exclaimed. "Your parents will expect you to submit to your husband, will they not?"

She thought of her indulgent parents and saw no difficulty. "I do not see why they should," she said confidently. "They have never constrained me to anything against my will. Sure, if I say I will not have him, they will arrange it. Why did I not think of this before? Oh, kiss me again, Robbie love me again! All will be well, I know it!"

★ ★ ★

Her confidence was misplaced. The Earl of Essex returned to England at the end of that month of November and the members of the Countess's immediate family were astonished at the hysterical scenes and uproars enacted by their indulged and petted younger daughter who would scarcely look at her husband, let alone go to bed with him.

"But this is ridiculous!" expostulated her mother, Lady Suffolk, facing her equally bemused husband across a table in the newly finished winter parlour of their great newly-built house of Audley End in Essex. "What maggot is eating her brain? They were married and the marriage must be consummated. Good God, the King arranged the match himself! You must talk to her again, Henry, and force her to obey."

"Force her? But how?" Lord Suffolk's face was puzzled and incredulous. "We have never forced her to do aught all her life long. What do you mean? That I should beat her? Is that your notion?"

It was Lady Suffolk's turn to look puzzled. "Well — no," she admitted lamely. "I cannot bear the thought of that. Dear me, I confess that I am at a stand. She stays shut in her room, weeping and refusing food — refusing even to lay eyes on poor young Essex who cannot imagine what has come to her. And it is so embarrassing for us all that he should be staying here at Audley End! It seemed such a good notion that they should have their first few nights here, under our wing, as it were. But who would have thought of this?"

"There is but one thing for it," announced Lord Suffolk, pushing back his chair and rising to his feet determinedly. "My uncle must speak to her. He is head of the family and has much influence with her. She will heed what he says. Thank God he is due to arrive here tomorrow."

He walked to the fire that blazed in the hearth, resting his arm on the carved stone mantelshelf, staring perplexedly into the flames, picking abstractedly at the diamond buttons of his blue velvet doublet, shadows and firelight dancing on the pale panelled walls behind him and flickering on the gold embroidery of his wife's rose-coloured kirtle.

"Well, I hope he has more luck with her than we have had," said that lady on a note of despair. "Is she ill, do you think? What is it with the child?"

"She says she is in love," replied her husband over his shoulder. "Did she not tell you?"

"Not a word. In love? And with whom, pray?" Lady Suffolk gave an exasperated laugh. "Oh, sweet heaven, what nonsense! She can have as many lovers as she pleases after the marriage is consummated and she has borne her husband a son and this she well knows. Who is the man who has caused this garboil?"

"It is Sir Robert Carr," answered Lord Suffolk with a resigned shrug, turning again to gaze into the fire.

"What? *That* puff-ball?" she cried in disbelief. "I doubt he knows what to do with a woman!"

"Oh, he knows well enough," said her husband. "He may accommodate His Majesty, but his instincts do not lie that way."

Lady Suffolk stared. "Did you know

she was mooning over him? I did not and so I tell you."

Lord Suffolk was then constrained to inform his lady of the plan devised by his uncle whereby Frances was to win Carr to her side for the benefit of the Howard tribe. "But 'twas not intended that she should go mad for him," he finished, shaking his head gloomily. "Nay, this was not in the plot at all."

"Well, since the idea came from your uncle, let him unravel the tangle!" declared Lady Suffolk roundly. "And, since it will be in his hands, we can leave all to him. It should all be settled by the end of the week if he has the handling of it, I am sure. Frances pays heed to him. Husband, ring the bell for candles to be brought; the room grows dark as pitch. Yes, we can safely leave the matter to your uncle," she repeated, raising her arms above her head in a long and satisfying stretch. "Let us have some wine, too. I am worn out with all this argufying."

When Lord Northampton arrived next afternoon, tired after a difficult journey from London in the cold and rain, he was not over-pleased to be greeted by a volley of complaints about his great-niece's extraordinary behaviour.

"For God's sake," he growled, "let me have my cloak off, a seat by the fire and a cup of hot wine before you overpower me with your moans and grumblings." He gazed round the chilly spaces of the Great Hall, at its elaborate carving, the richly wrought plaster madallions of the ceiling and shivered. "By heaven, this place is as draughty as a barn! Will the house ever be finished? The workmen have been at it six years and still it is not done." He glanced quizzically at his nephew. "Is it your intention to build a whole town here, Henry?"

"We do but wish to build a house that measures to our place in the world!" answered Lady Suffolk sharply. "After all, Henry is Lord Chamberlain, not a mere gentleman of the Court."

Lord Northampton uttered a sardonic snort. "Then your place in the world must indeed be a high one, Catherine, if it is to be measured by the amount of bricks and mortar you use! I pray God that Nephew Henry may sustain his lofty position, if only to support your pretensions. He might be ruined else. Now, what is this drama about Frances — and please do not speak both at once. My ears will not stand it."

He listened impassively to their woes, sipping his hot wine, his dark, lined face expressionless. When they had done, he said: "Very well, send Lord Essex to me, if he can be found in this half-done rabbit-warren."

At this, Lady Suffolk, who had no more love for her relative-by-marriage than he had for her, gave an exclamation of annoyance and tossed her head angrily before ordering a servant to find the Earl of Essex.

He came, wind-blown and slightly panting, a tall, aquiline, auburn-haired youth, whose good looks were marred by an expression of puzzled discontent.

"I am but just returned from riding, my lord," he explained apologetically, making his bow, "or I would have been here sooner. As you can see, I have come at once."

Lord Northampton looked the boy up and down. He seemed a handsome, strong lad, well set up, good enough for any girl, surely. "Well now, young man, what is it with you and my great-niece?" he demanded abruptly. "Have you done your duty by her in bed?"

Lord Essex gave an angry laugh and threw out his hands. "Done my duty in bed? How can I do it? She will not come near me! Ask Lord and Lady Suffolk, they will tell you."

"They have told me till my ears ring," remarked Northampton drily. "I wish to hear it from you. Have you spoken kindly to your wife, told her she is beautiful, said the things that females like to hear? Have you given her gifts? Kissed her?"

"Of course I have!" retorted young Essex. "As for kissing her, sir, I have tried, for she is very pretty, but she will not have it."

"Will not have it, indeed!" Northampton was contemptuous. "If she will not obey you, you must force her. She is your wife — it is your right."

Lord Essex blushed a painful scarlet. "You need not tell me my duty, my Lord!" he blurted out. "I know it well! But she scratched my face — see — and kicked my shins so hard, struggling so violently that I had to let her go. Then she ran from me and has stayed locked in her room ever since."

"Dear me," observed Northampton. "A pretty coil and no mistake. I will see Frances and speak with her. Let me have words with her privately; I am sure I can make her see reason. If not, perhaps we might try what a little starvation can do. I believe it to have a powerful effect upon the unwilling and obstructive."

Lord Northampton's interview with the recalcitrant Frances took place in that young lady's bedchamber. She was sitting in a chair near the fire, wrapped in a blue velvet bedgown, a sullen expression on her face which did not lighten as her great-uncle was ushered in. Stiffly he seated himself in a chair on the opposite side of the fireplace, stretching out his dark-veined hands to the warmth of the flames. There was a silence until she broke it.

"I know why you have come to see me, uncle, and I tell you at once that it is of no use."

"Come, come, my child," he said

smoothly, "this is no greeting! I hear that you are troubled. Will you not tell me your mind?"

Frances choked and sniffed and out tumbled the lovelorn tale amidst sobs and tears.

"But you have exceeded my command, have you not?" said Northampton when the story was told. "I ordered you to draw Carr to your side, not to fall in love with him yourself. You have made things very difficult for us all, Frances."

"But I love Robbie, uncle! I love him with all my heart and soul! I cannot and will not live with Lord Essex. I hate him!"

"Tut, tut, what a to-do!" Northampton stroked his chin meditatively. "I am sorry, my girl, but live with your husband you must and go with him to his estate at Chartley you shall. I order it."

"I won't, I won't! You will have to bind and gag me first! I will not go!"

"*Frances!*" Northampton's voice was like the crack of a whip. "Control yourself! How dare you behave so? Be silent at once and listen to me. That is better. You say you love Carr? Very well. Then act as other ladies do in such circumstances. Comply with our wishes with as good a grace as you may, be polite to your husband, bed with him obediently and I will see that you are oft at Court and able to meet the man you say you love. If not, we shall have to use methods other than verbal persuasion."

She stared at him defiantly. "I will not bed with Essex, persuade or threaten me as you will!" she cried.

"By the Cross, you are a fool!" he snapped, irritated at last by her obduracy. "Use what brains you possess, if you have any, which I doubt. We want no scandal in this family. No scandal, you understand? Now, hearken to me. I insist you bed with your husband and, what is more, it will take place here and tonight. No!" He raised his hand, silencing her cry of protest. "I will brook no arguments. I have told you my will and you will obey me, Frances, unless you wish for physical correction which I am perfectly ready to have applied. Your misfortune is that your parents have been too soft with you; a good beating now and again would have done you a power of good. I warned them often enough that by denying you the rod, they were making one for their own backs and see how right I was!" He heaved himself to his feet. "I will leave you now. Call for my servant to assist me downstairs, then dress yourself and make an appearance at supper." He held her angry, tearful gaze with his own. "Dare to defy me and I will have the servants carry you down as you are, in your bedgown, struggle and scream as you will. Remember it."

Sulky and glum-faced, she came down to supper and the evening passed without incident, until she discovered that her great-uncle had meant every word of his promise that she should sleep with Lord Essex that same night. At first, she wept, screamed and refused to yield, at which Lord Northampton rose with difficulty from his chair and dealt her a box on the ear that sent her staggering. Through the resultant uproar, Northampton's voice was heard asking if she would like another of the same and if so, that he was willing to give it her. Astonished and half-frightened at such treatment, her cheek scarlet, her ear throbbing, Frances decided to submit, though with a very bad grace. As events turned out, she arose in the morning with her marriage still unconsummated, poor young Lord Essex being so overcome at his rejection and so embarrassed at the outcome, found himself to his dismay and his wife's unconcealed derision, totally unable to perform his part.

"Well?" demanded Northampton of his niece, early next morning. "Are you now a wife in earnest, madam? I trust you have overcome your foolish reluctance."

Frances laughed triumphantly. "The answer is No!" she answered impudently. "He cannot do it." She gave her uncle a pert, challenging stare.

"He cannot do it?" repeated the old man. "What do you mean by 'it', pray? Do you presume to tell me that you, a supposedly virgin wife, know what is to do between a man and wife abed in marriage?"

"Yes, I do know," she replied, still smiling. "And he cannot do it."

"And how do you know?" he shouted. "Do you mean to tell me that some dog has taken your virginity? How dare you,

Frances? Who is the man?"

"Surely you realise that, uncle," she said with a shrug. "It is Sir Robert Carr."

In a rage, he lifted his stick and thumped it on the floor with a crack that made Frances flinch, for all her hardihood. "How dare you!" he roared. "So we offer Essex damaged goods! What if Carr had made you pregnant? What then, eh? And what will His Majesty say if he should discover that you have cheated the husband he chose for you and taken his favourite to your dishonoured bed? Ay, you may well look startled! We are like to lose the royal favour through your whorish ways — do you understand nothing, stupid? You deserve a good thrashing and I am minded to see that you receive one!"

Frances had lost her saucy air and taken refuge in tears. "But uncle, what is to become of me? I do not like or want Lord Essex. I think him a faddle, a noddy-cock."

Northampton was rendered temporarily speechless at this description of the unfortunate Earl of Essex and could only glare at the girl standing sobbing before him.

"A *faddle*? A *noddy-cock*?" he thundered, recovering himself. "Where have you learnt such lewdery? I am shocked, deeply shocked to hear such disgraceful words on a woman's tongue. I cannot think what has come to the younger generation to behave so. As to the condition of your husband's cock, I can do nothing about that, but you can and you will, my lady!"

"It is your fault," she countered defiantly, still sobbing. "'Twas you who said I must smile on Robbie Carr and I did so."

He thumped his stick again. "Sweet Christ, did I tell you to lift your skirts for him, to fall on your back, to act the doxy? No, I did not! You will stay with your husband as his wife, whether you like it or no. I have had enough of this ridiculous garboil and, as head of the family, I command obedience. Remember, ma'am, you are but a woman and have no rights. You are as much my creature and your husband's as any dog or horse and do not forget it! Now, get

116

out of my room and endeavour to make yourself pleasant to Lord Essex who has my entire sympathy. I have said my say and that is the end of the matter. Be off with you and remember that it is your place to obey!"

She flounced out, weeping loudly and slamming the door behind her. When she had gone, Lord Northampton grinned to himself. There went a bold little bitch, if ever there was one. What a boy she would have made! Nevertheless, she must conform as a woman should. The family must not be brought into disrepute, especially not by a silly girl.

And so the business rested.

It was all very unsatisfactory for Frances, for Lord Essex and Robert Carr. Lord Essex felt that his life had degenerated into a series of marital tests at which he constantly failed; Frances felt that her youth and beauty were being wasted as the contempt she held for her husband corroded gradually into an immovable hatred; Robert Carr found his position as royal favourite, which he had previously regarded with a casual, good-humoured cynicism, becoming increasingly distasteful and irksome as he thought of Frances day and night.

"I desire a normal relationship," he groaned to Tom Overbury. "But the King monopolises me and the lady I love is wed. It is a wretched situation and I would I were out of it, for my part."

"Faith, do not grow capricious now with the King!" exclaimed Tom, dismayed. "You need His Majesty's love, Robin. You must keep it, for if you go down, I go down with you. For God's sake, use your wits, man. Besides, you have grown used to luxury and soft living, with folk fawning upon your words, imagining you to be a sharp-brained political wizard."

"Oh Lord, do not remind me of that!" rejoined Robert. "That is another thing that worries me. My life is totally false, Tom. You write my letters to Lady Essex, they are *your* words that I prate, parrot-like, at Council meetings and added to this, I must act a part in the King's bed. Is it worth all the jewels and favour, Tom? Sometimes I view myself with consternation, I vow I do."

"Ah, you have a fit of the mulligrubs," said Thomas comfortingly. "You are in the dumps, that is all. What can we do that will cheer you? Shall we get up a masque, design costumes for it, write music for it? What do you say?"

Robert's eyes brightened. "Well, I cannot write music," he said doubtfully, "nor can I sketch, or think out a plot, but mayhap I could work out some notions for costumes. The Queen likes masques; perhaps this might cause her to look upon me with a little more favour." He smiled. "Ay, let us do it. It will serve to pass the time."

Robert's eyes were to brighten still more in the spring of 1610, for King James created him Viscount Rochester in March and he joined the ranks of the nobility who did not welcome him with any great enthusiasm, although being forced to admit that his supposed political wisdom and foresight were nothing short of formidable. In view of this, his peers decided that he merited their reluctant respect and treated him coolly but courteously enough. But for all his hypothetical power, for all his

119

presumed brilliance, for all the support he received from Thomas Overbury and the deep love of King James, Robert Carr, Viscount Rochester, was restless, unhappy and dissatisfied at this time. His feelings for Frances began to override his commonsense and he who had been a byword for good humour and equable temper, became touchy and irritable. Overbury grew at first concerned, then alarmed.

What had come over the sweet-natured Robin? wondered Tom. He gave the matter much thought. It was that plaguey woman, of course, that sly, whey-face cat of a Frances Essex. She was not of the type that Thomas admired when he did fancy a woman — so small and clinging, so fair and pale, with those large wistful grey eyes and, if Thomas mistook not, a will and resolution of iron under that fragile, delicate exterior. And of course Robin would be as putty in her little dainty hands, he having as much wit and insight as a maypole. Why he was even forgetting to honour the King with the respect that one in his position was due! If he continued so, King James might grow cool and then where would the new Viscount Rochester and Sir Thomas Overbury be? thought Tom, his heart giving a thump of apprehension. We would be in the dung-heap for sure, he said to himself dourly. Ay, that was where Randy Robin and Tricky Tom would end their days if Robin were not made to see the error of his ways.

So reasoned Sir Thomas Overbury, walking alone on the towpath by the river Thames at Richmond on a bright summer morning. And if Robin was discontented, so of a certainty was Tom! If Robin could be made a Viscount for nothing but empty-headed pretence and a few humpings in bed, then he, Thomas who was anything but empty-headed, surely deserved the same, if not more! Certes, he was not likely to get it and he knew why. He could read character too well, was too accurate in his personal opinions and far too sharp of tongue to be appreciated by any of the fools at Court. Moreover, His Majesty was woundy jealous of his friendship with Robin, viewing him with barely concealed dislike whenever he saw them together.

So I must keep Rob sweet, thought Thomas, walking by the river. It is vital that I do, for if not, we shall both lose all and that must not be.

5

ALL'S FAIR IN LOVE AND WAR.

Told by Frances, Countess of Essex.

1610 – 1612

EVERYTHING I did was for love of Robbie. No man was ever so loved by woman. There is nothing I would not have done to retain his love for me, yet it all came to naught in the end. As I lie here, riven with pain, in my lonely, sick and unsought bed in this quiet room at Grey's Court, I know that my miserable life will soon be over and I think and think of all that took place and my part in it. Not a good part, I fear me, but it was all for love, all for love . . .

I could not endure my husband, the Earl of Essex. He was pleasant, handsome and any lady's fancy but mine. Mayhap if he had taken me by force and continued to do so, I might have regarded him with respect, or even affection after a time — who knows? But he was only a lad; a lad with no experience of women and none of bed-sport, neither, so I despised him. How could he compare with my beautiful beloved, whose very hand upon me caused me near to faint with desire? Therefore, being young and unable to control my feelings, I viewed Lord Essex first with scorn, then with a dislike that soon turned to outright loathing. I was never a philosopher, never one to accept what I thought of as second-best, never one to be content with what I did not want — never one to compromise. Nor, during my life, had I been trained to make the best of a bad situation, having been given all I wanted, however foolish, until Lord Essex came home.

Then all was changed. My parents would pay no heed to my frantic pleadings and my misery, they who had previously granted my least wish. No matter how I sulked, screamed, stormed and railed, all was of no use. I was bound to my unwanted husband for life and no one would do aught to aid me. I was desperate as I sought in my mind for succour.

One dull grey day, some weeks after I had been constrained to live with my husband, I sat gloomy and snarling in his great, cold prison of a house at Chartley in far-off Staffordshire, when suddenly I bethought me of one who might help me. What of Anne Turner? She had aided me before; she might do so again! My frowns turned to smiles as I considered the matter. Lord Essex at that time was still attempting, though ineptly, to win my favour and, to achieve this, did his best to grant my wishes. Very well, I would express a wish. I would desire to go to Court. Nay, I would demand to go to Court! Once there, it would be a simple matter to seek out Mrs. Anne and tell her of my wretched troubles. So, soon enough, we were on our way to London.

We rested overnight at an inn to break our journey and, if it had not been for me, my Lord would have accepted inferior rooms, if you please! Essex was never one to put himself forward, but I soon settled all, securing the two best rooms in the place as bedroom and parlour. Why should not two married couples of low degree be turned out to make room for us? I saw no wrong or injustice in that — the creatures were mere clods of low degree — but Essex protested at this as though a robbery were being committed.

"They have paid for their accommodation," he said to me. "They should not be put out merely because you desire their rooms."

"Oh, what fustian!" I cried angrily. "I never heard the like! The best is our due and I have ever been used to nothing else. I tell you, here and now, that I will have those rooms and none other. Landlord, I am the Countess of Essex and I demand your best chambers instantly! Here is good gold," and I handed him a purse, "see that my commands are obeyed!"

He bowed and did as I wished, of course. What difference could it have made to two countrified yeomen and their fat wives to sleep in lesser rooms? The whole affair was nothing but fanciful nonsense on the part of my husband and

I let him know my feelings in good measure.

Once in London, we stayed in my sister Elizabeth's lodgings hard by the tilt-yard of Whitehall, she being away with her husband William, Lord Knollys at their estate in the country. We quickly made ourselves comfortable there and I lost no time in sending Lord Essex out and calling Mrs. Turner in. She was right glad to see me again.

"Oh God, my sweet Turner!" cried I, the greetings over. "How I am beset! My pesky husband is at me night and day and the dear knows I am sick of him. What can I do? And how is my dearest Robbie?"

I flung myself on the yellow silk day-bed that was placed in the bay of a window that looked out over the very tilt-yard where I had seen my precious love fall from his horse four years earlier. Then he was a mere squire in the train of his patron, now he was Viscount Rochester and a great man, deemed wise beyond ordinary in the ways of statecraft. I longed more than words could tell to see him, to hold him, to feel his kisses, his body — oh, saints preserve me, how I longed! — and here was I, tied to a stammering worm. It was unendurable and my existence as his wife stretched endlessly before me, caught as I was in this trap.

Mrs. Anne pulled a stool forward, near to the day-bed, and sat herself upon it. She looked very handsome this day, clad all in rich black satin with the lace collar and cuffs of yellow, having had her famous new starch used upon them, her golden hair in curls about her pretty face and fastened in a knot at the back of her head.

"No heir is expected then?" she asked, laughing.

"My faith, no!" I exclaimed. "Nor like to be, if I can avoid it."

She smiled, her blue eyes twinkling wickedly. "Has your lord been a lusty husband to you?" she enquired, her brows raised saucily. "Has he slept with you each night as an eager husband should?" And she giggled behind her hand.

"Do not tease!" I snapped. "It is no joke for me. I tell you he is useless. His member could not raise a handkerchief, let alone itself. It is good for nothing but piss."

"What?" she cried. "Dost mean it? I was jesting, merely. Does he not approach you, seek your love, fondle you? Not at all?"

"He did," I replied irritably, "but it did him no good, for I strove with him, bit and scratched him each time he tried."

She stared at me thoughtfully. "Why did he not ravish you then? Most husbands would."

"Oh, we struggled and he was the stronger, of course. But then his tent-pole collapsed and since then will not rise for aught and thank God for it say I! I pray it never will. Now, what of my Robbie? I have his last letter with me, Anne. It was brought to me at Chartley by secret messenger. There is nothing of the laggard about *him*, I do assure you."

"He is well and handsomer than ever," said Mrs. Anne. "He knows you are here and is afire to see you. Do you wish to meet him at my house? It can be arranged for a trifling fee."

Did I wish to see him! I yearned to

do so, felt I would die if I did not, so hot are the ardours of youth. And it was all arranged, smooth as silk, that we would meet at Mrs. Turner's cloaked and masked, the next afternoon, when my husband would be a-hunting with friends.

"So what shall we do about Lord Essex?" asked Mrs. Anne, staring about her at my gowns flung across the bed, at my furs tossed on the chest, at my jewel-box spilling its contents on to a table.

"What can we do?" I repeated hopelessly. "I do not know — you must answer that question."

"It is simple enough," she replied. "We must give him a potion."

I gazed at her, feeling a little fright, for I knew not what kind of potion this might be, or what effect it might have.

"Is it safe?" I asked nervously.

"Oh ay, never fear. His desire will be turned from you and he will cease to seek your love. He will remain as you say he is now — limp as a rag."

"Then I say Yes," I answered, taking a deep breath and making up my mind. "I will give you the money for it now."

"Has my Lady noticed that I am in black?" asked Mrs. Turner, taking several gold coins from my palm. "My old husband had recently died and I am now a widow. Therefore my means are straitened and I have to charge more for the medicines I make or procure. So I must beg you for two more gold angels, Lady Essex."

I believed her; why should I not? I had not then learnt of her lover who was keeping her in comfort. Besides, I had known her almost all my life and trusted her. I gave her the money she wanted and gave myself up to thoughts of Robbie. How I longed for the morrow, when he and I would be together abed, making love at Anne Turner's house! I could eat no supper that night, nor sleep and I was more ill-tempered toward Essex than ever. I could not understand how he came to be such a feeble-spirited ninny, for his parents were not fainthearts, nor his grandparents, neither. His father had been the rash and lusty Robert of Essex, the last favourite of old Queen Elizabeth who had chopped off his head for his wild ways, while his grandam was the famous Lady Lettice, some sort of cousin to the old Queen and hated by her for second-wedding the Earl of Leicester whom Elizabeth had adored. Lady Lettice was still alive in those days of my youth, red-haired and still very handsome, but my faith, what a tongue had she! It would have melted lead off a roof! I said little and behaved right meek and quiet when we stayed with her, for she was a formidable dame.

Then for a mother, my husband had the Countess of Clanricarde. She was the daughter of Sir Francis Walsingham, a most clever crafty statesman of days gone by. This lady was then alive also and although she was courteous to me, I do not think she cared for me overmuch. She had a very seeing eye, that lady, and I was relieved that we visited her but little, Essex disliking her second husband. I daresay she would have ferreted out all between Robbie and me and any hope of our meeting would have been at an end. So there were no weaklings in Essex's ancestry as far as I could tell, yet with me he was as water. I despised him utterly and let all know it, moreover.

I was unkind, I suppose, but I would not be different had I to live my life over again. I thought only of Robbie. Everything I did was for love of him.

So my dear lover and I met almost every day of the weeks that Essex and I spent in London. We were crazy for one another and Mrs. Anne kept our secret well. I think no one marked us, for I was always with Essex when in public and never so much as glanced at Robbie, nor he at me. And Anne Turner's medicines worked right well, for Essex became so discouraged in his efforts to act the husband that he wellnigh gave up any attempt in the end. So I was very pleased and felt free to act the wife with Robbie at any time I could. *He* was never limp as a rag, I promise you! He had but to lay eyes upon me for Master P. to rise up and salute! This made me blush when in company, but 'twas mighty exciting for all that and I think no one noticed such naughty stirrings but I, for who would suspect such a thing of the King's sweetheart? Mrs. Anne and I had many a giggle over it.

And yet I was dissatisfied. I wanted to

marry Robert, to be his wife in reality, to end my mockery of a marriage and to belong to my darling with the blessing of Church and law. I spoke to him of it and he wanted it as much as I, but had no notion of how to bring it about. It was an exceeding difficult matter and seemed but an impossible desire.

★ ★ ★

Three years passed in this wise. Three long years of anguish and rapture, love and loathing, at the end of which I felt much older than my nineteen years. Things seemed no further forward between Robbie and me, although our love was as strong as ever and our desire to be wed as firm. Robbie's hateful friend, Thomas Overbury, disliked the very air I breathed and made no secret of his distaste for me. He was jealous, of course, the horrid creature, and spoke ill of me to Robbie whenever he could. Well, no one could endure him, not even Lady Richmond, for whom he had a fancy. He made up to her with letters and poems and much good did they do him with her! She tore them all up — I saw her. So bitter-tongued and snarling as he was, only dear, sweet-natured Robbie would befriend him and I could not understand why he bore with him. He was handsome, I grant you; tall, dark and well set-up, but he seemed in a rage against all the world and all the people in it. Often would I question Robbie about Tom Overbury.

"Why do you keep him as a friend, darling? Why do you always defend his sneering ways? How can you remain friendly with one who hates me whom you love?"

But his answers were always evasive. I did wonder if Overbury meant more to him than merely a friend, but he swore that this was not the case — although I dare say Overbury would have had it so if he could! As it was, they quarrelled about me often enough.

The climax came late one winter night, after I had managed to visit Robbie secretly in his rooms, during a stay at Whitehall. We were tiptoeing along a dark gallery for me to reach my lodgings, I wrapped in a black, hooded cloak, when we heard footsteps approaching and

Robbie pushed me into the deep shadow of a doorway just as Overbury appeared round a corner, candle in hand.

"For God's sake, Robin!" he exclaimed. "What do you here at this time of night? Ah, you have been with that strumpet again! Will you never leave the company of that base woman?"

"That is enough, Tom!" rapped out Robbie, very angry. "I will not allow you to speak of her in that fashion. I love her and hope to marry her as you know full well."

"God's nails!" cried Overbury, breaking into a jeering snigger. "What a hope, indeed! You waste your time dwelling upon such moonshine. She will bring you only sorrow and misfortune; I know her kind. She is born to make trouble, that one, and will do you no manner of good. I have told you this often enough, the Lord knows."

"Ay, and you may cease to do so!" retorted Robbie sharply. "I am tired of your scolding and mean to go my own way in this. Remember it!"

"Have I ever offered you bad advice — come, have I?" Overbury's voice rose excitedly. "You are nothing without me; do not delude yourself, Robin! Very well, seeing you do so neglect my counsel, I will leave you to yourself to stand on your own legs!"

"Which I can very well do!" answered Robbie angrily. "We shall see if you are as necessary to me as you imagine yourself to be, my friend!"

"You are flown with pride," hissed Overbury, "and pride goeth before a fall and so *you* remember!" He stamped off in a rage, leaving Robbie grinding his teeth and me shaking with fury.

After hearing his opinion of me in so many words, I detested him more than ever and Robbie's feeling for him began to grow less and less, for who wishes to hear one's beloved so maligned?

To add to my discontent at this time, when all seemed to be turning awry for me, there was no merriment to be had at Court, neither, for the Prince of Wales had but just died and all were plunged into mourning. I was right put out by this, for I had hoped for plenty of distractions to take my mind off my worries, but the Prince was desperate ill

137

for some weeks before his death and the King so melancholy over it that there was no dancing, no games and no gaieties of any kind. It was as dull as ditchwater and I was bored to extinction.

As to the Prince himself, why, 'twas sad enough thing to take and die at eighteen years of age, but faith, he was of the censorious sort, forever casting a disapproving eye upon those whom he considered to have overstepped the bounds of what he thought right, and that scarcely included Robbie and me, so I did not miss his royal presence one jot, for all that he was so good-looking and so much admired. One has one's own feelings in these matters.

So, what with all this misery, together with Overbury's sharp dislike of me and the fretting to my nerves with my wretched marriage, I grew quite forstraught and melancholy myself.

At last, in desperation, I spoke to my great-uncle of Northampton. Until that time, fond though he was of me in his crabbed fashion, he had ignored all my pleas and protestations, but now he seemed disposed to listen to my case.

"You say that Lord Rochester truly wishes to marry you?" he asked me one January day while I was visiting him at Northampton House. He gazed thoughtfully into the fire for a few moments. "And how do you suppose such a thing might come about?" he went on, turning his head and staring at me, his hard black eyes glittering under frowning brows.

"I do not know," I said with a sigh. "But it is an honourable love, you see, and I do love him so much that I would give anything to be his wife."

"Tell me, has Essex entered you?" he barked at me so suddenly that I blinked. "Well, has he? Answer me, girl!"

"No!" I replied forcefully. "I told you so once, long ago. He cannot do it and never has." I almost smiled as I bethought me of Mrs. Anne's potions with which she had kept me well supplied, but managed to keep a straight and woebegone countenance.

"So, so, so. What then of Rochester? Are you still his mistress?"

"Of course I am," I said crossly, "and you know it well enough."

"H'm," said my uncle, gazing once more into the fire. "I have been thinking. A marriage to Rochester would be no bad thing, in fact. 'Twould bring us closer yet to the King and would be of much benefit to our family. It might be managed, I fancy, Frances, but mouths will have to remain shut and secrets close kept." He stared at me again. "Understand me," he said, "I have hitherto been very much for your marriage with Lord Essex, seeing that the King wished it in the beginning, but it seems to be a sorry affair, bringing naught but trouble and no heirs. If the matter be handled properly His Majesty may be brought to agree to an annulment."

"And what is that?" I queried, my heart beating fast with hope.

"A legal parting," he told me, "by reason of nonconsummation of marriage. There is one difficulty, however, and a great one."

"A great difficulty?" I cried. "Oh, can it not be overcome?"

He gave a sardonic snort. "Only if you are a virgin," he said.

I gasped in dismay and no wonder!

"But would folk not take my word, uncle? Surely — "

"Folk might," said he, "lawyers will not. And you are certainly no virgin, are you, my dear great-niece?"

"But who is to say? Why should I not be believed?"

"Because you will have to be examined by a party of matrons, Frances. Therein lies our difficulty."

I burst into tears. I had been raised high to hope and now was dashed down into despair. The case was hopeless; I could see no answer to the dilemma and sobbed aloud.

My uncle banged his stick on the floor as he always did when annoyed. "Cease that snivelling!" he snapped. "I have a notion that might serve. The fault with you, Frances, is that you leap to conclusions. Now, hold your noise and pay attention to me. Of course we cannot let you be examined; that would set all to naught. But there are some, I make no doubt, who would volunteer to take your place for a sufficient reward."

I gave a shriek of joy, rushed forward and kissed him heartily on both wrinkled cheeks. "There, there, that is enough," he grumbled, looking pleased for all that. "You have dislodged my cap and disarranged my cape, so excitable and silly as you are. Get away, girl, for mercy's sake, and do not utter a word of this to anyone as you value the success of the plan."

"Not even to Robbie, uncle?"

"Well, of course *he* must know, stupid! He will give wrong answers else. But impress upon him that he must be silent on the subject of your virginity, or lack of it, if he wishes to wed you."

So, once back at Whitehall, I spoke of all this to Robbie who was as excited as I to think that we might have a chance to marry.

"My faith," he said, laughing with pleasure, "Tom will be surprised, for he thinks we have no chance at all."

I seized his arm. "Oh, sweet Jesus, you must not breathe a word of this to Overbury!" I exclaimed. "Why, he knows that you and I are lovers and that I am no virgin, therefore. He hates me, Robbie and you know it. There is to be a legal hearing in order to dissolve my

142

marriage to Essex and do you truly think that Overbury will keep his knowledge to himself? He longs to rid you of me and what a weapon this would be to his hand! No, you must not tell him."

"I had not thought of that," said my darling, looking crestfallen. "But he is bound to learn of the hearing, is he not? What is to keep him quiet?"

I shrugged my shoulders and threw out my hands in a gesture of anxiety and ignorance. "Oh, Jesu, I cannot imagine! I will talk to my uncle and see if he has a notion. He is very clever, Robbie. I am sure he will have something in his mind."

"I hope you are right," replied Robbie, moving restlessly about the room from chair to window and back again. "It is such a pity that Tom has taken so much against you, sweetheart, for he has been a loyal friend to me. But you come first, my darling, and if Tom is against you, he is against me too. And yet," he said, with a sigh, "I am sad that he and I should be so at odds. It seems that I must see less of him."

See less of him! thought I. See nothing

of him at all, for my money. Aloud, I said: "Oh, he is best out of our way whilst all this is afoot. My uncle will settle matters, I am sure."

And he did. He explained all to His Majesty. All, that is, except my lack of that desirable commodity, virginity, and the King was only too pleased to agree to the suggestion that Sir Thomas Overbury be offered a diplomatic post in some foreign country. I was highly amused to learn of this 'offer' when he told me the details of it.

It was while I was with him again at Northampton House, that I heard how he had had audience with the King and reported to His Majesty that Robbie had quarrelled with Overbury and had decided to cool the friendship. King James was delighted to hear it.

"God's life, my Lord!" he cried. "This is good news indeed! That Overbury is an arrogant, sour devil of a fellow and for my part, I canna abide him. Nor can the Queen. She says he is insolent and knows not his place. I agree with her. Now is our chance tae see the back o' the man."

"Would Your Majesty consider a diplomatic post for him?" asked my sly old uncle. "In foreign parts, of course."

"Och, o' course!" rejoined the King with a laugh. Then, slapping his thigh: "Hey, I have it! He can go as Ambassador to the Court of Muscovy!"

At this they near burst their sides with merriment, so my uncle told me, grinning to himself at the memory of it.

When I asked Why so? he explained that to be given such an Embassy was not advancement, far from it. It was exile and everyone knew it for what it was.

"'Tis a neat way to be rid of the troublesome wretch," he said, chuckling, "and if he refuse to go, why then His Majesty will send him to the Tower instead, as a punishment for disobedience, so either way we are clear of the fellow."

I gazed at him with admiration as he sat there before the fire in his small oak-panelled winter parlour, the weather being iron-cold, his leg up on a cushioned stool, his black velvet robe furred with sable falling in folds about his wizened frame, a black woollen cap with earflaps pulled well down over his bald head. He was very old, being then full seventy-two years, and with a bad leg, but his wits were as knife-sharp as those of a young man.

"Will he refuse, think you?" I asked hopefully.

"For sure he will. He will see the appointment for what it is and will refuse it, you can take my word on that."

And all turned out as he said. He was a marvellous cunning man, my great-uncle. Sir Thomas Overbury refused the Embassy with haughty indignation and on the twenty-sixth of April 1613, was clapped into the Tower for his pains. So he was well out of it and I could breathe easy, I thought. Good old King James seemed very happy for me to wed with Robbie. All he wanted was for his darling and mine to be happy and, provided no other *man* stood in the way, felt no jealousy at all, which I took as a very good omen.

"Oh sweetheart," I said to Robbie before Essex and I left Whitehall for a wretchedly tedious visit to Chartley, "Matters go our way at last. Is it not beyond all wonderful? And I am so glad that Overbury is out of the way so that he cannot poison your mind against me."

"He could never do that!" answered Robbie hotly. "Never. For all that he tried hard enough," he added.

"I tell you," I said earnestly, "if he were still at Court I would never get my annulment and you and I would never wed."

"Oh, I know it well," he nodded. "All the same, it is hard that he should be in prison."

"You are too soft-hearted," I told him fondly. "He brought it on himself you cannot deny that. Besides, it will not be for long, I daresay."

"No, I am sure it will not," agreed my lover. "There can be no reason to confine him long and even though the King likes him not, His Majesty is not unjust. No, I expect that once the legalities are over and we are safe wed, Tom will be free again."

Suddenly it occurred to me that Sir Thomas Overbury might not be silent even though imprisoned. This made uneasy thinking. I would have to ponder the problem, but at the moment my mind was taken up with the parting from Robbie.

"You will write to me while I am stuck at Chartley, will you not, dear heart? I cannot tell you what your sweet letters mean to me."

Did a slight shade pass over his beautiful face when I said this? I could not be certain. I repeated my question more urgently.

"Ah, of course I will, my love," he assured me, kissing me passionately. "I will do my best to write whenever cares of state permit, but do not fret if you do not hear from me quite so often as heretofore, for I will have much to do since Tom is not by me to act as my secretary and ammanuensis."

And so we parted.

It was as well that he had warned me of a lack of letters, for they were few indeed and nothing like those he had been used to write to me. I grew distraught, thinking him to be growing cold, and fretted myself greatly about it. Indeed, I quite lost my appetite and became pale, nervous and very bad-tempered as a result. After our stay at Chartley I was only too glad to leave there to go to Audley End and spend some time with my parents, but I felt no better there and was often in tears, to my mother's concern.

One bright morning, soon after May Day, I walked with my mother down to the little river Cam, where it ran busily between its green banks at the front of the great house.

"What in the world is it with you, Frances?" she demanded, glancing worriedly at my glum countenance as we strolled over the grass, our skirts brushing the heads of the daisies and budding buttercups as we went. "Surely you have everything to make you smile now, daughter! Lord Northampton will be certain to see that you are freed from your marriage since he favours you so greatly. Why do you look so melancholy?"

"Oh, it is because Robbie does not write to me so oft and I am feared that — "

"By Our Lady!" interrupted my mother,

her blue eyes round with dismay. "Do not tell me that he grows cool now! Not when your great-uncle is moving heaven and earth to get you your way! Have you slighted Lord Rochester in any fashion?"

"No, I have not!" I snapped, twitching my arm free from her anxious grasp. "I love him and he knows it."

"Have you then seemed too fond, too loving? This can sometimes — "

"I tell you *No!*" I shouted, stamping my foot so that the damp riverside grass soaked my white satin shoe. "There — now see what you have made me do! These slippers are brand-new and one is ruined; it is too bad! For God's sake, what would you, Mother? Would you follow Lord Rochester and me about with a book of rules in your hand, groaning: '*Smile at him now, Frances,*' '*Kiss him now, Frances*', '*Go to bed with him now, Frances*'?

For answer, my mother raised her hand and slapped my cheek none too gently. "Go to, daughter!" she cried angrily. "You are right shrewish and unmannerly. Since you are so evil-tempered, I will go within and you may stamp and yell out here alone." As she walked away, she turned. "And I am sorry for Lord Rochester if you behave so with him!" she called over her shoulder as a parting shot.

"A fig for your sorrow!" I shrieked rudely after her. "I care not what you feel for me or for Robbie, so now!" And I marched up and down, kicking uncaringly at the grass, so that both my shoes were spoiled, sobbing and wringing my hands in a fine frenzy, the skirts of my green silken gown growing wet and muddy as I flung about the river-bank. This made me angrier than ever and I ran into the house, locked myself into my bedchamber and penned a long, hysterical letter to my great-uncle, entreating to hurry the business on.

He arrived at Audley End some two weeks later, his servants carrying him in from his gilded, curtained litter like an aged baby and setting him down in a carved oaken chair in the Great Hall, he calling irritably for cushions, wine, his stick and a footstool. These being brought, he snatched his gold-topped stick, grasping it in his dark-veined old hand.

"Frances," he said sternly to me as I curtsied before him, "I begin to find you a pesky nuisance. If it were not that I am a little fond of you, I would not bestir myself in your amatory affairs. Here am I, plagued with agitated letters from you, from your parents, from Lord Rochester, being sent messages every day from his Majesty, and all because you cannot live peaceably with your lawful husband and Sir Thomas Overbury sees fit to refuse an honourable post abroad! I tell you, I am growing too old for all this garboil and for any journey but the shortest. However, now that I am here in this half-built labyrinth, I mean to stay for a se'ennight or two. I cannot endure a return to London too soon, my bones and my health will not bear it."

Catching the expression on my mother's face, concealed too late, he let out one of his snorting laughs. "Ah, my dear Catherine," said he, grinning at her maliciously, "I regret to grieve you, first by abiding a while beneath your imperfectly tiled roof, and secondly by thus holding my approaching death at bay a little longer. I am therefore foisted upon you, my Lady."

My mother's cheeks were bright with an angry flush and her lips tightly compressed, but she managed to say: "You are very welcome, my Lord," in tones that all too obviously gave him the lie. She detested him, did my mother. He knew it and cared not a straw, leaving no opportunity undone to tease and taunt her, the old rascal.

"We are in a great pother about Frances's affairs — " my father began, but Lord Northampton cut him short.

"There is no need for any pother," he announced decisively. "I have seen to it that the Lieutenant of the Tower, Sir William Wade, has been replaced by Sir Gervase Elwys. I have done Sir Gervase many a favour in the past and now is his chance to return them by doing as I wish. Indeed, I have instructed Sir Gervase to depute a certain Richard Weston to act as Overbury's personal attendant."

"Who and what is this Weston, uncle?" I asked. "Is he reliable?"

He gave me a very straight look. "I do

not choose creatures who are unreliable," he declared. "Weston is an under-keeper; he will do as he is bid and keep Overbury close during his imprisonment. So you can rest easy, my girl, and more easy still, for your cousin Katherine Fiennes, has agreed to act as your substitute during the examination for virginity."

"Good God!" exclaimed my father. "What a business is this! How in the world did you persuade Katherine, uncle?"

My great-uncle laughed again, a hoarse, grating snicker of a laugh it was and rubbed the two knotted fingers of one hand suggestively against the thumb. "Money, nephew," he said. "Good solid English gold. It hath great powers of persuasion as we all know. Ay, Katherine will do it."

My father drew a deep breath. "I fear we may be stepping into deep waters," he murmured. "Let us hope we do not get a wetting."

"You will not while I live," answered Lord Northampton, "and I do not intend to perish yet, not even to oblige your wife."

Looking at the old man, I was conscious of a feeling of doubt. He looked ancient enough to give up the ghost at any moment. I prayed he would not do so for a year or two at any rate; at least, not before Robbie and I could wed.

And that thought brought Robbie to the forefront of my mind. "You said you had received letters from Lord Rochester, uncle?" I asked him, suddenly remembering. "Why should he write to you when he does not write to me?"

For once my kinsman seemed slightly at a loss. "Ah — as to that — I will speak to you of it in private," he said, after a moment. "Come to me after dinner and I will enlighten you."

I went, and what he told me gave me such a shock that I felt first nigh turned to ice, then to flame with fury and outrage, for *Thomas Overbury* had written those love-letters to me; Thomas Overbury had filled those pages with false passion; Thomas Overbury had known all my secrets and I was ready to die with the shame and humiliation of it. I stared at my uncle in horrified silence for a long space, then I screamed and screamed and screamed so that he was forced to call for assistance, saying that I was in pain by reason of having eaten somewhat of sour peaches badly pickled. He did not betray me, for which I was grateful.

It seemed that Robbie, in desperation without Overbury to aid him, had confessed his lack of skill as a penman to my uncle, imploring his secrecy and indulgence in the business of Overbury's invention and scholarship, and my uncle, half-amazed and half-amused, had agreed to keep silent. I felt as though rolled in the mire; I felt I could kill my uncle as well as Robbie and his abominable friend with my own hands. I insisted upon leaving for London there and then, with or without my husband.

"My sister will make room for me in her lodgings!" I cried, beside myself. "Elizabeth will have me. I must see Robbie — I *must*!"

And they let me go, no doubt thinking my brain had turned. I did not care.

Once in London, after much weeping, wild accusation and desperate explanation, the miserable matter was resolved and

Robbie and I were heart to heart again. But oh, although I could forgive my darling, I could not forgive that misbegotten snake of an Overbury. How could I? What woman could? I prayed that Richard Weston would keep him close as an oyster so that naught against me might be spoken for, at a word from him, I would lose my all and never, despite all my great-uncle's machinations, would I ever marry my beloved Robbie.

6

WHERE THERE'S A WILL,
THERE'S A WAY.

1613 – 1614

AS might be expected, Lord Essex was not best pleased when informed that the forthcoming separation from his wife would take place upon the grounds of non-consummation of marriage by reason of his impotence. The walls of Audley End fairly rang with his furious protests.

"Do give heed to me, my Lord," said Lord Northampton one fine bright day, when the young man had stamped into the comfortable, south-facing, sun-filled room allotted to the old man during what had turned out to be a long stay. "If you will cease your bellowings and listen to me, you might profit just a little from my words. Do you love my niece?"

"I tell you, I am not impotent!"

158

shouted Lord Essex wrathfully. He paused, realising Northampton's question. "Love Frances? No, I do not!" he answered emphatically. "She has led me a wretched life and my health has suffered because of it, I am certain. I am even more certain that I am not impotent. It is just that when I am with her — oh God Almighty!" he cried, rather wildly, "I am at my wits' end with all this! Would I were a free man!"

"Then pay attention to me," repeated Northampton. "Events can be put in train to dissolve your unfortunate marriage if — and I say *if* — you can suffer being branded as impotent during a legal hearing, so that my great-niece may prove herself a virgin."

Lord Essex burst into a loud satirical laugh. "A virgin? God's teeth, how may she prove herself to be what she is not, my Lord? She has been playing the whore with Lord Rochester these last three years and although I have had no luck with her, he has, for sure! But I am not impotent! My powers are as good as those of any man."

"Oh, send me patience, I will take your

word for that!" snapped Northampton. "You can prove your precious powers to the world after your marriage is dissolved. Now do you understand me, boy? Let yourself be supposedly impotent for the hearing only and I do assure you that you will be freed from an unpleasant union, able to wed whom you wish and to father as many children as you have the strength to do. As to my niece's equally supposed virginity — that is all arranged. Think well, my Lord, take what time you need and let me know your answer. I must tell you that the hearing will proceed whether you agree or not and the marriage *will* be dissolved. Such matters can be contrived. However, should you agree to my argument, the whole affair will go through without too much fussation and as quickly as the Commissioners will allow."

Lord Essex walked to the window and stared out, the sun gilding his chestnut hair and turning the yellow satin of his doublet to shimmering gold. Suddenly he turned, a determined expression on his good-looking young face. "Very well," he said, "I will do it." He set his chin. "It will be almost worth it to be rid of Frances," he said quietly, "but I promise you, sir, that as soon as I am free, the world shall know full well that I am as other men. I shall not cease to prove it."

Northampton nodded. "I do not care what you do once the marriage is declared null and void. You may re-populate London if you have a mind." His hard old face relaxed in a wintry smile. "I do feel for you, my Lord," he said. "Never think I do not. But one sharp pain to your self-esteem may bring about a lifetime of happiness to follow. You will keep silent — it is understood?"

"You have my word," answered Lord Essex. Frowning and biting his lip, he bowed and left the room as Northampton spoke his thanks.

* * *

The August day was very warm and although the windows of a room in Lambeth Palace were set as wide open as possible to catch every breeze that might find its way in from the river

161

Thames, the atmosphere in the chamber was stifling and the Commissioners, who had been appointed in June to try the nullity case between the Earl and Countess of Essex, were uncomfortable indeed, wishing themselves anywhere but indoors. The hearing had dragged on, day after day, week after week and the good Commissioners were growing weary of the heat and the seemingly interminable discussion. There sat His Grace Dr. George Abbot, Archbishop of Canterbury; the Bishops of London, Coventry and Lichfield, together with two Chancellors of the Exchequer, Sir Thomas Parry and Sir Julius Caesar. There also fidgeted Sir Daniel Dunn, the Dean of the Court of Arches, seated beside Sir John Bennet, while next to Sir John were placed Dr. James and Dr. Edwards, two doctors of law, whose fur-banded black robes were almost insupportably hot and heavy.

"God's wounds!" whispered Dr. James to Dr. Edwards, earning a minatory glare from the Archbishop. "I begin to melt away!"

"Hush!" murmured Sir John Bennet.

"His Grace of Canterbury is about to speak. Pray heaven he do not maunder on."

His Grace the Archbishop rose to his feet, casting a quelling eye upon his fellow Commissioners. "Gentlemen," he boomed, his rich sonorous voice resounding into every corner of the stuffy room, "as you are aware, we are here to adjudicate upon this case of nullity brought by the Countess of Essex upon her husband the Earl, who has declared himself to be bewitched, finding himself to be impotent with his wife only and not with other women."

"This is news after eight weeks dissertation?" mumbled Sir Daniel Dunn wearily. He leaned toward Sir John Bennet. "What will you wager that the lady will somehow manage to prove herself virgin?"

This caused Sir John some trouble in concealing a snigger, raising his hand to cover his grinning mouth as the Archbishop went on with his speech.

"Now I would impress upon you, my good sirs," intoned His Grace, "that during the past weeks of our deliberations,

I have been in correspondence with the King touching the unpleasant topic of witchcraft thus raised by Lord Essex, mentioning my doubts that it could cause impotence in any marriage, but His Majesty desires the case to continue. It seems that His Majesty wishes this marriage to be nullified," continued the Archbishop, twisting his long face into an expression of grave disapproval, "and I make no comment upon it — "

"Thank heaven for that," whispered Dr. James without moving his lips.

" — merely to remark," droned His Grace, unconscious of undercurrents, "that should the Countess be found to be virgin, then a verdict of nullity must be given. The King has, therefore, in his kindness, deputed the Bishops of Rochester and Winchester to assist us. Let us welcome them, gentlemen!"

As the Bishops entered the room, there was a general shifting and movement in order to make a space for the two stout clerics who squeezed themselves in and sat down with difficulty.

"Come, this should hurry the business on," said Sir John, under cover of the resultant bustle. "Now we can be assured of a nullity verdict, so long as we do not die of overheating before the tedious matter is done with. I will not take your wager, Sir Daniel. It is certain that the Countess will be virgin, come what may."

"We have already endured two months of wordy vapourings," answered Sir Daniel with a resigned sigh, "and it seems like to continue for ever. For my part, the lady may be as pure and untouched as she wishes."

The gentlemen were right on both counts. The hearing did continue, if not quite for ever, certainly for another five weeks, when the result of the Countess's examination finally settled it. The veiled lady presenting herself for the examination by a group of twelve matrons was undoubtedly virgin, and the puzzled, but unsurprised Commissioners were delighted at last to be able to pronounce the marriage null and void.

Frances was free to remarry.

"Now we need be secret no longer!" she cried rapturously to an equally joyful Robert at Whitehall. "Now I bless my cousin Katherine for taking my place! We can wed at last — we can be together for always. Oh, I am in heaven, are not you, Robbie?"

For answer, Robert kissed her again and again. "And now that you are free," he said, smiling happily, "mayhap Tom might be released from prison. He cannot hurt us now."

At the mention of her enemy's hated name, Frances flushed scarlet. "He can *never* hurt us!" she cried. Then, noticing Robert's enquiring frown, she said: "I mean he can never hurt us while he is where he is — behind locked doors. Set him free and he would whisper lies and malice about us, sure as fate, sure as death!"

"Oh darling, do not speak so wildly." Robert drew her down beside him on a cushioned settle. "Poor Tom has paid for his meddling, although I own 'tis pleasant to be free of his constant reproaches and overwatching. He had become a trifle wearisome with his everlasting lecturing, I will admit. Perhaps, after we are safely married, His Majesty will set him at liberty, for he has done us no harm, in spite of your fears."

But Robert was to receive a severe shock before many weeks were out, for the news came that Sir Thomas Overbury was dead, had died in his prison of what was thought to have been an obstruction in the bowel.

"Or it may have been the dysentery," Northampton told the anguished Robert. "At all events, it was a malady of the guts. Of course, the Tower is never healthy in the summer and these infections go straight to the belly. It happens time without number and there seems to be no cure. Most unfortunate," he said, "but in the midst of life we are in death, as the clergy constantly tell us."

Struck to the heart with regret and compunction, Robert agonised over the death of his comrade and for that, although he was never to be popular or even liked at Court, at least he was commended for showing loyalty to a friend.

"My God!" he groaned to Frances, head in hands. "I feel the veriest swinish varlet! I could have spoken to the King against his imprisonment and His Majesty would have heeded me! Worse than that, when Tom wrote to me from the Tower, imploring my help, I answered that I was doing my best to obtain his release, while all the time doing nothing — nothing! And now he is dead. I tell you, I feel like a liar and a murderer."

Frances was conscious of a strong feeling of impatience. To wail in such fashion over an unpopular, cunning and spiteful knave who were best dead and out of the way, seemed to her to be an access of sentimentality. Could not Robbie understand this? It seemed he could not. Of course, the creature had been his great friend — men were so odd in their friendships, thought Frances — and Robbie had a warm and loving heart, so she would bite back her annoyance and endeavour to humour him.

"You must not feel so, dear heart," she crooned. "No one could guess that he would die before his time; 'twas God's will, my dearest. Your sorrow does you credit, but you would have lost him as a friend anyhap, once we were wed. You know how he hated me. Well, at least you are spared seeing him detest your wife, are you not? Come, have good cheer, think of our wedding and let us be merry. We are to have our heart's desire and should be right thankful for it."

"Ay, you are right," sighed her lover. "He is gone and no amount of mourning will bring him back. I would not wish to mar our happiness by too much repining, my love, so I will do my best to put sad thoughts behind me as you advise." He straightened his shoulders and smiled at her. "Only think, darling, a few short weeks more and we shall be man and wife! It is like a miracle. How can I not be happy at such a prospect?"

Soon after this, on the 3rd of November 1613, King James created Robert Carr Earl of Somerset in preparation for his wedding and after the ceremony remained alone with his favourite.

"Och, ma sweet Robbie," murmured His Majesty, stroking the young man's jewelled hands, "no one can wish ye happiness more than I do. May your life wi' that little lassie be one of unending joy."

"Oh, that it will be, Sire," answered

169

Robert suffering the King to load him to an alcove lit by a tall window of stained glass which threw coloured patterns of red and blue over them as they sat. "I have no doubt of it."

"And will ye not call me 'Dad' again, darling? It warms ma heart when ye call me so. No more of formality — we are alone now. Let it be 'Dad', ma dearie." He embraced Robert with great fervour. "And ye willna forget your old Dad when ye're wed, will ye? I'm fair unhappy without ye, Robbie, so pray dinna forget, dear laddie."

★ ★ ★

Frances and Robert were married on the 26th of December in the Chapel Royal at Whitehall with much pomp. They made an outstandingly good-looking pair; she in white satin powdered with pearls, her mass of golden hair loose under a pearl and diamond wreath as befitted a virgin, causing repressed titters, raised eyebrows and imperfectly concealed grins, to which she, having realised her ambition, paid not the smallest heed. Robert, also in white satin, his long red hair curled and glowing, his small russet beard combed to a modish point, diamonds blazing about his tall person, made a god-like groom, his heart beating with excitement and pride.

He had come far, he thought, as he knelt at the altar, the Archbishop's prayers resounding about him scarcely heard. From a younger son of countrified Ferniehurst to a knighthood, then to the Viscountcy of Rochester and a place as a Privy Councillor, next, a position as Secretary to the King, to be followed by the Earldom of Somerset and marriage to a lady of the noble and influential Howard family and one who was counted the most fascinating woman in England. Pretty well for young Robert Carr, once considered to be something of a dullard! Ay, and the King ate out of his hand; he could do as he would with the King. Pretty well indeed, thought Robert Carr, Earl of Somerset, kneeling at the altar on his marriage-day.

He had climbed high and would go higher yet. Ay, a dukedom could be next, with power and possessions without end.

His future stretched before him, rosy as the dawn, golden as the sun at noonday. He forgot that a sunset could also be of gold and rose, but why should he remember this? His star was risen, he was but twenty-seven years old, at the height of his manhood and prideful beauty, while the lovely girl at his side was still only twenty, his adored one and as good as she was lovely! Why, he thought, one had only to gaze upon the perfect face, into those limpid grey eyes, to know that Frances Howard was the nearest thing to an angel that one could find upon this old earth. Ah, he was a lucky fellow, reflected Robert Carr in the Chapel Royal upon his marriage-day.

7

RIDING FOR A FALL.

1614 – 1615

IN the weeks and months that followed his marriage, the new-made Earl of Somerset's private life was ideally happy, but his public life was growing increasingly troubled. His delighted absorption in his beautiful young wife and consequent neglect of King James caused His Majesty to begin to look elsewhere for affection, scarcely noticeably at first, but the King had become all too aware that his beloved favourite had less and less time for him, seemingly taking the royal love for granted. James was hurt, feeling slighted and deserted. He had given Robbie everything, had raised him high, put his heart into the young man's keeping, loved him, trusted him, allowed his marriage and now, after all this, was enduring snaps and snarls, irritability, bad temper and neglect. James, miserable and deeply wounded at his darling's defection, began to notice the presence of another beautiful young man at Court, a certain George Villiers, tall, strong, dark-eyed and auburn-haired, who was being slyly put forward by Robert's enemies, jealous of his riches and position and weary of his ever-growing arrogance.

Since his marriage, Robert had begun to feel all-powerful, confident that ill-fortune could not touch him, nor disaster threaten him. Having now a constant and normal love to satisfy his physical urges, he became resentful and impatient of the demands made upon him by His Majesty and chose to forget that the rather pathetic, middle-aged monarch was the continuing source of all his good fortune. As time went on, his lofty confidence became slightly eroded by the fact that without the presence of Tom Overbury he was finding political matters increasingly incomprehensible, a state of mind not eased by the fact that others were beginning to notice this and remark on it. Troubled, he grew more irritable and short-tempered than ever, struggling to push his uneasy thoughts to the back of his mind and ignore them as resolutely as possible, telling himself that such notions were naught but a pack of fanciful nonsense. Was he not the Favourite, the King's dearest love who could do no wrong?

At this point he always smiled to himself at what he deemed his foolishness. The King was his puppet, everyone knew that, so why should he worry? He was secure enough — 'Old Dad' could refuse him nothing; never had and never would. As for that puppy, George Villiers, who was prancing around the Court nowadays, why, Robert could send him to the right-about whenever he wished to do so! Villiers was merely a passing fancy, a novelty once noticed, soon forgotten. A penniless nobody — a time-server — he knew the type well enough. His Majesty would never be fooled by such a spine-bender, so the matter was not worth another thought, decided Robert scornfully, sauntering through the galleries of Whitehall Palace, toadies at his side, servants at his heels, his head held high and haughty.

★ ★ ★

Six months after Robert's wedding, in full summer, the old Earl of Northampton died at the age of seventy-four. The tumour in his leg had grown bad enough to kill him as he lay in his fine mansion near the Cross at Charing. Frances wept at his death, for she felt she was bereft of a protector and Robert was conscious of some concern at the loss of a political flat adviser, a rough and somewhat bullying adviser, it was true, but one he could not afford to be without, especially since he had now been given the post of Lord Chamberlain by the King in an effort to keep him sweet. This meant that he was placed above the two Secretaries of State, Sir Ralph Winwood and Sir Thomas Lake, elderly statesmen of immeasurable experience, who could barely endure the sight of Robert Carr, Earl of Somerset. Now that Lord Northampton, with his powerful and scarifying tongue had been gathered to his fathers, the enmity of the two secretaries had free rein.

"See'st thou, my good Thomas," said Sir Ralph to his colleague, after a stormy session in the Council Chamber when the Earl of Somerset had stamped out of the room in a tearing rage, "that upstart Carr is but an ignorant dullard, for all his fine talk and conceit. He knows naught of state matters and yet is put over us. I tell you, it infuriates me."

Sir Thomas, leaning forward in his chair, rested red-velvet clad elbows on the long table in the now-deserted Council Chamber and nodded in agreement with his friend. "I am fair puzzled," he said, "to know how the creature was able to fool us all into thinking him wise in statecraft. He is a ninny, Ralph."

The grey-haired Sir Ralph hitched himself on to the edge of the table and gave a bark of laughter. "You are puzzled? Faith, I am not! Why, the fellow is a real sawney suck-eggs, as the country folk say — all fart and no bowels. See, he was wise only when Overbury was at his side, was he not? So soon as Overbury was prisoned, the vaunted political powers of our pretty faced wizard began to decline, did you not mark it? Now that Overbury is dead, he grows more of a dunce by the day. We may even bring him down eventually, who knows?"

"My stars, you are right!" Sir Thomas's bearded face split in a great grin. "And now that cunning old Northampton is croaked at last, Carr has no defender. We have him at our mercy — naught to fear from that quarter! God's wounds, what a jest! We may amuse ourselves as we will with the stupid fellow."

And, laughing heartily, the two gentlemen left the Council Chamber arm-in-arm, mightily pleased with themselves.

The situation did not please the Earl of Somerset. It wrought upon his nerves and made him more irascible still, even rousing the warm-hearted, mild-tempered King to quarrel with him. At last, the angry scenes between them grew so frequent and to such a pitch, that His Majesty, pained and greatly grieved, wrote his Robbie a letter.

. . . You have, in many of your mad fits, it ran, *done what you can to persuade me that you mean not so much to hold*

me by love as by awe, and that you have me so far in your reverence that I dare not offend you . . . I leave out of this reckoning your long creeping back and withdrawing yourself from lying in my chamber, notwithstanding my many hundred times earnestly soliciting you to the contrary . . . What shall be the best remedy for this? I tell you, be kind. But for the easing of my mind and consuming grief, all I crave is that in all the words and actions of your life, you may never make it appear to me that you never think to hold grip of me but by mere love and not one hair by force . . . I told you twice or thrice, you might lead me by the heart and not by the nose . . .

Dashing the tears from his eyes, the sorrowing King James continued his letter.

. . . As God is my judge, my love hath been infinite towards you, he wrote swallowing a great lump in his throat. *Let me be met, then, with your entire heart, but softened by humility . . . Hold me by the heart, you may build upon my favour as upon a rock that shall never weary to give new demonstrations of my affection*

179

towards you; nay, that shall never suffer any to rise in any degree of my favour, except they may acknowledge and thank you as a furtherer of it . . .

He paused, considering his words. He was warning Robbie; he must warn Robbie before the breach that was growing between them grew too wide to heal. Young George Villiers was a charming youth, ever ready with comforting and soothing words, tender, appreciative. Did not Robbie understand that his King might turn his love elsewhere? After all, reflected James miserably, I may be warm-hearted and tolerant, but I am not a worm to be trodden under-foot. I am a King, too, and Robbie must not forget this. He sighed, shaking his head mournfully. Oh, Robbie, Robbie, how I have loved you! There was nothing that I would not have done for you, given you, and even now would do if only you were kind to me again, my Robbie.

Taking up his quill pen with its brave green feather, His Majesty scribbled on.

Thus I have now set down unto you what I would say if I were to make my testament. It lies in your hands to make of me what you please — either the best master and truest friend, or, if you force me once to call you ingrate, which God in heaven forbid, no so great earthly plague can light upon you!

He paused again. Surely that was strong enough? Surely Robbie would not ignore that! Only a fool would do so. Well, I have but little more to say, thought James sadly, so I will draw my writing to a close and hope that my warning be taken.

In a word, you may procure me to delight to give daily more and more demonstrations of my favour towards you, if the fault be not in yourself.

There, he had done. Signing the letter, folding it and sealing it, King James summoned a servant to take it to the Earl of Somerset's apartments. When the man had gone, he laid his head on his arms and wept, for his heart was very sore.

In his sumptuous room, Robert received the King's note, opened and read it, brows raised, a hard, obstinate expression on his handsome face. Reaching the end, he tossed it carelessly aside, making an impatient sound in his throat and calling for wine and comfits.

He did not heed the warning.

★ ★ ★

So matters went on for another year until St. George's Day, the 23rd of April 1615, when young George Villiers received a knighthood at the hands of his King. Robert was a little put out at this, but not unduly so. After all, a number of men were knighted and for little enough reason. What was one among so many? He saw small cause for concern. What did concern him was his difficult position as Lord Chamberlain over an increasingly derisive and mocking Court. Shout and bluster as he would, fewer and fewer men seemed disposed to take him seriously, nor did they come to him, begging for favours as formerly. He wished that the King would notice his troubles but the old fool appeared to have but little time for him these days. So much for all those protestations of love, fumed Robert. A King can be as fickle as an ordinary man when all was said and done, although, he reminded himself, he could call the silly old bugger to his side whenever he wished; of course he could! He had but to crook a finger and the King would come running. The thing was, he was utterly sick and weary of being pawed about and drooled over by the old muttonhead and that was the sum total of it, but he supposed he should let himself in for another bout of kissing and fondling before too long — it might be only sensible to do so. At this point in his meditation, he shrugged. Ah, why worry? There was time enough for that.

In spite of his efforts to disregard all danger signals, he was infuriated when Sir George Villiers arrived at his rooms, sent there by His Majesty, to offer his services to the Earl of Somerset. Sir George had been a little dubious as to his reception by the Earl, but the King had hastened to reassure him.

"Dinna fret, sweetheart," he had said. "My Lord will be your patron; of course he will accept ye — 'tis the custom that he should. I expect him to do so; 'tis my wish and he knows it well."

So Sir George, trusting His Majesty's word, duly presented himself and went on one knee to His Lordship of Somerset, comely head gracefully bowed in ritual subservience.

"My Lord," he said respectfully, using the form of speech required by protocol, "I desire to be your servant and your creature and shall desire to take my Court preferment under your favour and your Lordship shall find me as faithful a servant unto you as ever did serve you."

The blood rushed to Robert's head. That this pipsqueak should come begging his preferment and sent by the King, no less! It was not to be borne! It was an insult, a calculated insult, raged Robert, quite forgetting that the request was in full accordance with courtly behaviour and not at all extraordinary. By God, he would not endure it! This conceited bantam-cock should return whence he came, with a flea in his ear for good measure!

"Be my servant, would you?" he roared, barely able to restrain himself from aiming a kick at the young man kneeling before him. "I tell you, I will none of your service and you shall none of my favour!"

Villiers, astonished, glanced up into the furious face above him. *Oho*, he thought shrewdly, *the King will not like this, or I am a Dutchman! Methinks my Lord of Somerset is riding for a fall.*

"And what is more," continued the wrathful bellow, "I will, if I can, break your neck — and of that be confident, jackanapes! Now, get you out of my sight and stay out!"

Rising to his feet, George Villiers said no word, departing with as much dignity as he could muster, to tell King James of his rough reception in carefully diplomatic terms. Left alone, Robert cast himself into a chair, his mind in whirl, too enraged for sensible thought. After a while he began to walk moodily about the lavishly appointed room.

Nothing had gone right since Tom's death, he said to himself — nothing, that is, but his marriage and Tom would have stopped that if he could. Now, as well as all the troubles under which he was suffering, there was this scurrilous verse that he had discovered upon his games-table just before the entrance of the Villiers popinjay. Who had dared to write such hateful rubbish? He took the crumpled paper from his pocket, smoothing it out and glaring at the hastily-scrawled lines with angry, disbelieving eyes.

I.C.U.R (I see you are)
Good Monsieur Carr
About to fall.

About to fall, indeed! fulminated Robert. Not if he knew it! He would like to get his hands round the neck of the dog who wrote this filth . . .

*U.R.A.K (You are a Kae)**
As most men say,
But that's not all!

U.O.Q.P (You occupy)
With your annullity
That naughty pack
S.X.Y.F (Essex' wife)
Whose wicked life
Hath broke your back.

*A jackdaw in peacock's feathers

186

Suddenly, with a strangled sound of fury, he tore the paper across and across into tiny pieces and flung them from him. How dared they? How dared they! And with Frances pregnant, too! Thank God she had caught no glimpse of this foul verse. Poor angel, it could go fair to bring on a miscarriage!

He was glad he had taken the house in Islington village where she might rest and breathe the fresh country air, away from libidinous gossip and scandal. He would leave Whitehall and go there now, with a fig to 'Old Dad' and his faithless Kingship! Let him cavort with that creeping toady of a Villiers, if that is what he preferred! He would soon tire of the crawling lickspittle and come whining back to his Robbie. Meanwhile, his Robbie would reside a while at Islington without saying where he had gone. *That* would teach His Turncoat Majesty a lesson, raged Robert, swinging a tawny velvet cloak about his broad shoulders and calling for his horse and baggage to be made ready.

8

TRUTH WILL OUT.

October 1615

DURING all this time, Sir Ralph Winwood, Secretary of State and no admirer of the Earl of Somerset, had not been idle. Quietly and secretly, he had been investigating the circumstances of Sir Thomas Overbury's death, about which many rumours were being whispered in the Tower of London. He had spoken to the old Countess of Shrewsbury, a fellow-prisoner of Overbury, detained for her work in aiding the secret marriage of her granddaughter, the Lady Arabella Stuart, cousin to the King and a claimant to the throne. Lady Shrewsbury, while in the Tower, had heard some interesting conversations of a nature that she was eager to impart to Sir Ralph. He had noted down all her information and sought for more.

He was not to seek long.

Before the summer had quite passed, Sir William Turnbull, the English Ambassador to Brussels, had arrived in London, hotfoot to see Sir Ralph Winwood, with some very urgent and confidential news for that gentleman.

"Come in, come in, my good Sir William!" cried Sir Ralph, all eagerness, at the door of his rooms in Whitehall. "I hear you have some particular information for me, concerning a Certain Secret Matter. Let us go into my private cabinet where none can overhear a word we say. You will take wine? Cakes? A piece of fruit?"

Declining these delicacies, Sir William had prefessed himself wishful to confide instantly in Sir Ralph. "This is for your ears alone," he said, following his host to the little private inner room. "I will take refreshment later, when I have unburdened myself. You will open your eyes when you hear what I have to say."

And the tale he told made Sir Ralph gasp. It appeared that a certain young Englishman named William Reeve had been taken mortally ill in Brussels but a short while back. Realising that death was near, Reeve had begged to be visited by the servants of the English Ambassador, for his conscience was sorely troubled with a state secret that he must confess for his peace of mind and hope of heaven to come.

"Well, well, what said he, what said he?" cried Sir Ralph, avid with curiosity. "Is it evidence? True evidence?"

"You shall judge when you hear," answered Sir William. "For my part, I think it to be so. Reeve told my people that he had been apprenticed to a certain Paul de Lobell, an apothecary. This de Lobell sent Reeve to the Tower with instructions to administer an enema to Sir Thomas Overbury. Reeve did so and Overbury died the next day."

"Jesu! Was the enema poisoned?" queried Sir Ralph breathlessly.

"Of a certainty. Reeve said that he was bribed to poison the enema with mercury sublimate, but stressed that de Lobell knew nothing of that."

"God Almighty, you are sure of this, Sir William?" Sir Ralph could

190

scarcely contain his excitement. He had felt certain for months that Overbury's death had been unnatural and here was vindication indeed.

"I do but tell you what my servants repeated to me, Sir Ralph," replied the Ambassador gravely.

"And did they also tell you who bribed Reeve to poison the enema?" Winwood enquired, clenching and unclenching his hands and biting his lips as he waited tensely for the answer.

"They did. Reeve said it was — " Here, the Ambassador leaned forward to whisper a few words into Sir Ralph's willing ear.

There had followed a complete silence as the two statesman stared at one another, one with the calmness of certainty, the other in blank amazement.

At last Sir Ralph Winwood spoke. "You will say nothing of this," he said, low, to the Ambassador, "and nor may your servants, you understand. There must be no word about it until I have collected all the evidence available. It is a state matter, you realise. There will be a trial, of course."

"Indeed, Sir Ralph, and I shall be happy to speak there if needed. Criminals must be brought to account. You may trust me and my household to keep silent."

"You have my heartfelt thanks, Sir William," the Secretary of State had assured the Ambassador — "I am more grateful to you for your timely and righteous assistance in this horrid matter than I can say. You have aided justice this day."

Soon after this, Sir Ralph Winwood might have been making a journey down river to the Tower to interview its Lieutenant, Sir Gervase Elwys, who had been appointed by the influence of old Lord Northampton. Alighting from his barge, he made his way across the landing stage and into the confines of the great palace-fortress. The day was dull, the wind chilly for September and Sir Ralph was glad to go within and warm himself beside the bright fire in Sir Gervase's comfortable lodgings. He had already decided upon his approach to the Lieutenant of the Tower. He meant to take a chance and trust that Sir Gervase would tumble out all he knew, to take him by surprise. If he were to hold his tongue, then Sir Ralph would have to seek for further evidence, so a strategy of shock might well prove efficacious.

"Now, Sir Gervase," he said gravely, a portentous frown creasing his brow. "I must tell you at once that you would be well advised to speak and clear yourself of the suspicions that have come to me concerning the manner of the death of Sir Thomas Overbury, who was a prisoner here."

Sir Gervase started violently, a scarlet flush overspreading his face to make his high colour higher still. "Oh my God!" he exclaimed nervously. "I knew that something would come out about that at some time! What can I tell you, sir? What is it that you wish to know?"

"All that you can tell me," replied Sir Ralph in tones of measured solemnity. "Hold nothing back, for the matter is of the utmost seriousness and I hope that you may not be too deeply implicated."

Sir Gervase gasped. His colour faded, leaving his cheeks ashy-pale. "It — it was like this — " he stammered, swallowing and clearing his throat convulsively, " — not long after I was appointed here, certain delicacies were sent in to Sir Thomas Overbury."

"Well, there is nothing strange in that," said Sir Ralph. "What next?"

"These delicacies were tarts and jellies," went on Sir Gervase. "I thought they would make a pleasant addition to the prisoner's diet." He swallowed again. "But before they could be taken to his table, they — they — "

He hesitated, looking worried and confused.

"Go on, man, go on," commanded Sir Ralph sternly. "What of these jellies?"

"They turned black!" burst out Sir Gervase.

"They turned *black*?" repeated Sir Ralph, astonished.

"Yes, indeed they did. Whereupon I threw them away and sent Overbury different, wholesome foodstuffs. Did I do wrong? Should I not have sent other foods?"

"Never mind that. Tell me more of this business. I wish to hear all about it."

"Oh ay, there is more!" rushed on Sir

Gervase, eager now to unburden himself. "There was a fellow called Richard Weston, an under-keeper, especially charged to look after the prisoner — a surly, silent fellow — "

"Yes, yes, never mind his manners!" urged Sir Ralph. "What of this fellow?"

"I caught him mixing poison with the prisoner's food," said Sir Gervase, "from a phial that he had and — "

"Well, what did you do then? Come, speak up, man!" Sir Ralph was impatient.

"I prevented him and threw the contaminated food away," answered Sir Gervase, staring at Sir Ralph as though mesmerised.

"And who gave Weston the poison? Do you know?"

"Yes, it was Mrs. Anne Turner."

"What!" cried Sir Ralph. "The starch-woman? The widow who is mistress to Sir Arthur Mainwaring? She who invented the famous yellow starch?"

"The same," replied Sir Gervase. "And this was not the only time," he added. "There were several more attempts which I forestalled."

"But the last was successful, was it not?

What have you to say about that?"

"Well, you see — " Sir Gervase looked about for support, and finding none, continued unhappily, " — you see, the prisoner was in the care of Dr. de Mayerne, the King's physician, but when the Doctor went from London to accompany the Court into the country, he left Sir Thomas Overbury in the care of a countryman of his, a French apothecary."

"And the name of that apothecary?" demanded Sir Ralph.

"His name was Paul de Lobell."

"*Ah!*" Sir Ralph felt a surge of triumph. The evidence was beginning to piece itself together. "And then?"

"de Lobell had a servant called William Reeve," went on Sir Gervase, "and it was whispered, after the prisoner had died, that Reeve had been bribed to give this enema. I saw no reason for an enema at the time, no reason at all, but William Reeve said that his master had instructed him to give it for an obstruction in the prisoner's bowels."

"And Overbury died," said Sir Ralph, his voice heavy with meaning.

"Yes, early the next morning, after a night of such agony I hope never to witness again," answered Sir Gervase, pale and remembering.

"And who gave Reeve the bribe? Do you know that also?"

"I believe it was Mrs. Anne Turner," answered Sir Gervase, "but I am not entirely certain of this, it being hearsay only."

Sir Ralph held the hapless Lieutenant in a long, thoughtful stare. "Can you tell me why you kept silent? Why did you say no single word as to what was afoot?"

"Well, I did not know what to do, Sir Ralph. I was in a difficult position. I was recommended for this post, you understand, and it was a great, though happy surprise to me, for until then I was almost unknown, with no friends at Court. It was Sir Thomas Monson, a fellow Lincolnshireman, who gave my name to the Earl of Northampton and he — "

"It was the Earl of Northampton, then, who finally secured you the appointment was it?" interrupted Sir Ralph, his voice sharp with eagerness. "And why did

197

he do that, if you were unknown at Court?"

"I have no notion," answered Sir Gervase lamely. "The thing was," he added, "that although I knew of the attempts to poison Sir Thomas Overbury, I dared not speak, for I thought that no one would believe me and that I might get into grave trouble for slandering great people without being able to give proof of my accusations."

Sir Ralph nodded. "Well, you are in grave trouble now, sir. I feel you should know that, through your silence, you have made yourself an accessory to the fact of murder."

Sir Gervase, horror-stricken, leaped to his feet. "My God! My God!" he cried. "That cannot be so! Why, I prevented many murder attempts myself! It was not my fault that Overbury died when he did! I did all I could to prevent it!"

"Nevertheless, the fact stands," declared Sir Ralph, "and I must inform you that you are now under arrest."

And the unfortunate Sir Gervase, half-fainting, was led away under his own guard to one of his own dungeons.

★ ★ ★

After these revelations, Sir Ralph decided that he had enough firm evidence to lay before the King who was thunderstruck, refusing at first to believe a word of it.

"And Northampton was implicated, ye say?" he cried incredulously. "Och, man, it canna be true!"

"All too true, I fear, Sire," was the answer.

"And it is true then, also, what ye say about the man Reeve's confession in Brussels?"

"The Ambassador himself told me, Sire," affirmed Sir Ralph.

"Then, if Northampton was in it, Robbie must have known — ! Na, na, I canna credit that! Why, Overbury was his great friend. Ma Robbie would have naught tae do wi' such a terrible thing!"

"Nevertheless, Your Majesty, the Earl of Somerset is implicated. I do not see that it can be otherwise. As you say, he must have known."

"But, Sir Ralph, do ye not comprehend," put in the King, after reflection, "that this entire dreadful matter could have been a fabrication put about by Robbie's enemies to destroy him if they could?"

"Oh I do, Sire, but surely it should be investigated? I have put Sir Gervase Elwys and Richard Weston, the under-keeper, under lock and key, pending such an enquiry. I hope I have done as you would wish."

"Ay, I suppose ye have. But ye maun put it all in writing, ma good sir. Do that and I will appoint a Commission to look into the matter. I can do no less. But I canna believe Robbie to be aught but innocent, Sir Ralph. That he should be tainted wi' suspicion of such a thing is incredible, impossible!" His eyes filled with tears. "I know him, ye see. It is not in his nature to kill. God's wounds, what a fearfu' thing is this!" His face quivered and he turned his head away.

As a witness of the King's horrified misery, Sir Ralph felt sincerely regretful. But what would you? he thought, with a mental shrug. It was necessary for the poor old boy to know all the dark details and the sooner the better. After all, murder was murder and could not be condoned, no matter who the victim or the culprit. Oh Jesu, the King was weeping! Hey-day, it could not be helped. The whole affair was mighty unfortunate in every way, reflected Sir Ralph, bowing himself out unheeded. That is to say — he corrected himself with a grim smile — unfortunate in every way but one, for no matter what became of that swollen-headed windbag of a Robert Carr, his day was done. The man was finished. And after the trial was over, Sir Ralph Winwood would be ready to wager any sum that the arrogant Lord Somerset, if still retaining his thick head upon his overdressed shoulders, would be arrogant no longer, favourite no longer and, if ever released from prison, where he would undoubtedly be sent, seen about the Court no longer.

In common with most of his colleagues, Sir Ralph would be only too delighted to see Robert Carr down in the mire and utterly dispossessed.

★ ★ ★

As soon as the details of the murder plot had been set down in writing, King James appointed a Commission, of which Lord Zouche, Sir Oliver St. John, Sir Thomas Parry, Sir Fulke Greville and Sir Ralph Winwood himself were to be members. He had recovered somewhat from his emotion upon first hearing the story and was able to conduct himself calmly.

"Now, gentlemen," he said gravely to the Commissioners, "I will have ye remember that there be two things in this case tried and the truth can be in but one of them. First, whether my Lord of Somerset and my Lady were the procurers of Overbury's death; or, that this imputation hath been practised by some to cast an aspersion on them."

"What, my Lady too, Sire?" asked Lord Zouche, surprised.

"Of a certainty," answered the King, "for if my Lord be involved, mayhap he told my Lady of it. It is possible. Remember, I want this business to be investigated thoroughly. We want no mistakes in a matter such as this. Too much hangs upon it."

Leaving the palace, the Commissioners betook themselves straight to Whitehall Stairs, where they hired a boat to take them to the Tower to conduct a strict examination of Richard Weston. Eager to escape the horrid prospect of torture, Weston confessed his guilt and in so doing, implicated the Countess of Somerset. After this, the King could do no more than to hand the whole matter over to the Lord Chief Justice, Sir Edward Coke, leading to the interrogation of over two hundred people, a mighty task. After this, the King was forced to command a trial.

Immediately, at dawn of the next day, Sir Ralph Winwood and his fellow-Commissioners, took water at Westminster for Henley-on-Thames in Oxfordshire where they disembarked to meet with a company of soldiers especially sent ahead from London. From Henley they rode swiftly through the rolling, tawny, October countryside to Greys Court, the home of Lord and Lady Knollys with whom the Earl and Countess of Somerset were staying.

Upon their arrival at the stately, compact, three-gabled house, set so commandingly upon its rounded hill, the Commissioners were conducted to the first floor, where the Long Gallery ran across the east front of the mansion. Here, the tall, dark, dandified Lord William Knollys, brother-in-law to the Countess of Somerset, received his unexpected visitors courteously, but with a good deal of surprise, bidding them be seated and enquiring their business.

"Our business is with Lord and Lady Somerset who are, I believe, residing with you at present, my Lord," announced Lord Zouche. "We would also wish to interview a Mrs. Anne Turner who is here in attendance upon the Countess. Is it possible for us to have speech with them in private? We are on an assignment from His Majesty."

"With a company of soldiers?" asked Lord Knollys in astonishment, having caught a glimpse through a window of sunshine gleaming on polished helmet and pike in the courtyard below.

"An escort merely," put in Sir Fulke Greville quickly. "And, good my Lord," he cautioned his host, "we would desire you not to mention to Lady Somerset that we have business with Mrs. Anne Turner. This is by order of His Majesty and may be a little troublesome."

Lord Knollys stared at his uninvited guests in bewilderment, slowly turning to unease. "You would wish to interview Mrs. Turner here?" he asked at last. Then, struck by an unwelcome thought: "Or elsewhere, perhaps? That is to say — if there is trouble — " His voice trailed away.

"I see you take my meaning," answered Sir Fulke, relieved. "Is there somewhere where we may put a few questions to her? It is vitally necessary, my Lord."

"Ah — there is the Wellhouse . . . " said Lord Knollys dubiously, after a moment's thought. "I suppose . . . yes, it is fairly out of the way — out of earshot, if that is what — " He paused, looking worried, then gave a resigned shrug. "Well, I will send Mrs. Turner to you at once then. You may rest assured that I will say no word to Lady Somerset or anyone else, but by my faith, it is very strange — very strange indeed." Shaking his head, he withdrew and the Commissioners were left alone.

"Now," said Sir Ralph Winwood, as soon as the door had closed behind

Lord Knollys, "do you Fulke, and you Thomas, take Mrs. Turner to the Wellhouse, wherever that may be, and question her closely. Use any pretext. You know what to say when you have her alone and how to go about frightening her out of her wits. I do not anticipate too much difficulty with her. Lord Zouche, Sir Oliver and I will deal with the Earl and Countess, whose information should prove very interesting."

When Anne Turner came into the Long Gallery with a dancing step, her pink silk gown rustling, her golden curls bobbing, Sir Fulke rose to his feet and made her a gallant bow.

"Well met, Mrs. Turner," he exclaimed, with false heartiness, "I am right glad to see you. I am came with these gentlemen on business, but since you are here, I will ask you for more of your yellow starch. We are run out of it at home and my wife would never forgive me if I had seen you and not asked you for the recipe."

"And I also," spoke up Sir Thomas Parry. "I too am a petitioner for the famous starch. We cannot get enough of it. I count myself fortunate that you are residing here, Mrs. Anne!"

Mrs. Turner, curtsied, laughing. "Oh, I must not let you have the recipe," she said. "That would never do; but I have some starch here if you would like to take a little to your ladies, with my compliments."

"Excellent!" cried Sir Fulke. "Come, Mrs. Turner, let you and I and Sir Thomas walk outside and discuss your much-desired commodity while the others drone away at their dull state affairs. Did I not once hear from Lady Knollys that there is a famous well here that is over two hundred feet deep? There is? I have a fancy to see such a well, have you not also, Sir Thomas? Will you take us, Mrs. Anne?"

"My gown is hardly fit for a visit to the outbuildings," she giggled, "but how can I resist two such handsome and persuasive gentlemen who are so thoughtful of their wives? Come, I will show you the well, if you insist upon seeing it. It is through the gate on the south side — come!" And still laughing, she led the way out of the gallery.

"That was right neatly done," said Sir

Oliver as soon as the door shut after Mrs. Turner and the two men. "Will they be successful, think you?"

"Not a doubt of it," replied Sir Ralph. "A few twists of the arm or the wrist and she will give up her secrets easily enough. I know the type. No moral stamina, gentlemen. You will see."

As he spoke, the Earl of Somerset appeared at the further door of the gallery, richly clad as ever, his green satin suit ablaze with jewels, a look of indignant curiosity on his face. Polite bows were exchanged, then Lord Somerset snapped; "Well, what is it? You cannot see my Lady. She is resting and I will not have her disturbed. Give me your message and be off."

"Just so, my Lord," answered Lord Zouche pleasantly. "We would wish to speak with you first, anyhap, to enquire about a matter that has come to our notice."

Robert's haughty, irritable expression deepened. "And you trouble me with it here?" he demanded angrily. "You take a good deal upon your shoulders, gentlemen!"

"It is state business, my Lord," explained Sir Oliver St. John gravely. "State business?" echoed Robert. "And you wish to see my Lady? What kind of state business is that?" Receiving no answer, he shrugged and sat down with an air of exaggerated patience. "Very well," he said, with a loud sigh, "what is this precious affair that must be dealt with, no matter how it inconveniences me?"

"It is touching Sir Thomas Overbury's death, my Lord," said Lord Zouche quietly.

The interested eyes of the Commissioners did not fail to notice the tell-tale flush that mounted instantly to the Earl's fair brow at the mention of his friend's name, nor did they miss the sudden start he gave.

"Tom Overbury's death?" he queried sharply. "What of it?"

"Do you know how he died, sir?" questioned Sir Ralph Winwood.

"No!" exclaimed Robert crossly. "Of course I do not know the precise manner of his dying! What do you mean?"

"I mean that his death was not natural, Lord Somerset." Sir Ralph leaned back in his chair, the better to observe the effect of his words.

"Not natural? What is this? Do you mean that he was murdered? I do not believe it!"

"Nevertheless, it is true," replied Sir Ralph. "Sir Thomas Overbury was done to death by poison."

Robert stared at the three grim faces confronting him. "Tom, murdered?" he cried, aghast. "Sweet Jesus, who killed him? Who killed poor Tom? My God, if I could but lay my hands upon the creature who did it, I — "

"Come, come, my Lord," broke in Lord Zouche, "this pretence of ignorance is all very fine, but it will not do."

Robert jumped to his feet. "It will not do?" he repeated furiously. "What will not do? How dare you address me so, sir? Apologise immediately, or it will be the worse for you!"

"Pray have done with these heroics, my Lord." Lord Zouche was unimpressed. "We are here by order of His Majesty, commissioned to examine all concerned in the murder."

Robert shook his head in bewilderment.

"But this is nonsense! How can I be concerned? I know nothing about it."

"I should tell you, my Lord," drawled Sir Ralph Winwood, "that the under-keeper, Richard Weston has confessed all."

"That may well be so," answered Robert, "but I know of no such person. Why should I? I do not understand what you are about. I will bid you good-day, gentlemen." He began to move to the door. "My servants will see you out."

"Not so fast, my Lord!" said Sir Oliver. "His Majesty has commanded that you answer our questions. He has commanded it, sir, do you hear? Now, we must insist that you tell us all you know of Sir Thomas Overbury's death."

"I know nothing of his death!" cried Robert, goaded. "All that I do know is that he is dead, that he was my greatest friend and I miss him more than I can say. Now, if you will excuse me, I will leave you." Once again, he moved toward the door.

Lord Zouche leaned forward. "A moment, Lord Somerset. You could have obtained Overbury's release — it was in your power. Why did you not, since you say he was your greatest friend?"

Robert turned abruptly, biting his lips, the scarlet flood mounting again to his hairline. "I — that is — my head was full of the nullity case — " he faltered, unable to conceal his guilt and shame at the remembrance of the shabby treatment he had dealt to his friend at a time when that unhappy gentleman had needed him most.

"Exactly so, my Lord." Lord Zouche's contempt and suspicion showed in his face. "You found Lady Essex more interesting than your friend, I dare say."

"You have no right to speak so!" shouted Robert, firing up. "How dare you mention my wife in those terms! How dare you mention her at all? You may take your leave and go from here!"

"I fear not, sir." Lord Zouche was unmoved. "That is not in our power. As we have told you repeatedly, we are here by order of the King and I must say that I find it difficult to believe that you know nothing of this murder."

Robert seated himself once more. "I

am at a loss to comprehend you, Lord Zouche. Of course I know nothing about it," he stated emphatically, beginning to realise that there was nothing for it but to answer these astonishing questions.

"No one consulted you?"

"Consulted me? About what?"

"My Lord, it is for these gentlemen and me to ask the questions," said Lord Zouche, polite but firm. "Did anyone consult you over the matter of Sir Thomas Overbury's death?"

"No, they did not! Why should they?"

"Why should they not? You were close enough to the affair. I believe you to be concerned in the murder, Lord Somerset."

"You are mad! Raving mad!" roared Robert. "And so must the King be, to send you on such an errand!"

"Take care that you do not speak treason to add to the suspicion of murder!" warned Lord Zouche. "You had best guard your tongue, Lord Somerset."

Robert struck his hands together in exasperated amazement. "Pray will you tell me, without any further prevarications, just how I could be involved in the murder of my friend? It is ludicrous, I tell you! I demand an explanation."

Here, Sir Ralph raised a hand. "Since you appear to be in such ignorance, my Lord," he said smoothly, "I think the Countess might give you that. It seems to me that we should request her presence." And, as Robert made to protest: "It is by the King's command, sir."

Struggling to restrain his feelings of outrage and fury, Robert sent a servant for Frances and when she entered the room, childishly lovely, wearing a loose violet robe, her mass of shining hair tumbling in curls past her waist, the Commissioners, sophisticated men though they might be, were struck anew by her artless beauty. Robert sprang to her side and, with a protective arm about her, led her to a chair, for she was heavily pregnant.

"Sweetheart," he said gently, "these gentlemen are here, commanded by the King, to ask you some questions about poor Thomas Overbury." He noticed her sudden flush, followed by an extreme pallor and felt anxious about her health. "I pray you, sirs, to have a care. The

Countess is in a delicate condition."

What followed next was to make Robert think that he was living through some frightful waking nightmare.

"My Lady — " began Sir Ralph Winwood, then broke off as Sir Thomas Parry and Sir Fulke Greville re-entered the gallery. He glanced at them, brows raised questioningly, and received a nod in reply. "My Lady," he continued, turning back to Frances, "the game is up. We know of all your doings in the matter."

Snow was no whiter than her face as she gasped for breath. Silencing Robert's furious objections, Sir Ralph spoke again. "My Lady, we know that you commanded Mrs. Anne Turner to obtain poisons, that you paid her well to obtain them, firstly from Dr. Simon Forman wherewith to render your first husband impotent and secondly, from the apothecary, James Franklin, to administer to Sir Thomas Overbury with intent to kill him."

"*No!*" The scream burst from Frances's ashen lips. "No! No!"

"It is useless to deny it, my Lady.

The man Richard Weston and the man Franklin have confessed. They both tell the same tale."

"They lie!" she shrieked, turning wildly to Robert, who stood as one turned to stone.

"They do not lie," declared Sir Ralph remorselessly. "Sir Gervase Elwys has spoken also."

"He lies!" she wailed desperately. "He is mad!"

"I see." Sir Ralph paused. Then, swiftly, "And does William Reeve lie too?"

"Who is William Reeve?" she cried. "You are trying to trick me! To make me say — "

"To make you say that you know full well of William Reeve, Lady Somerset? Oh yes, indeed I am," pursued Sir Ralph, his voice hard. "Listen to me and listen well. Mrs Turner has confessed that you paid for the mercury sublimate that was put in the enema given to Overbury on the night before his death and that you also paid her to bribe Reeve to do this and to administer the enema. We needed only her corroboration and now we have

216

it." His voice rose. "She has but just now confessed, my Lady!"

"And what said this Reeve? Tell me that!" cried Frances, her voice shrill, her head thrown back in a frantic attempt to brazen it out. "Ha, you cannot, for he is in Bruss — oh God!" She clapped a hand over her mouth, realising that she had betrayed herself.

"Jesus Christ!"

With that smothered exclamation, Robert staggered to a chair and collapsed in it, shaking, head in hands, his stomach heaving, his vision blurred with shock. The voices about him echoed as from a sounding board as he heard, to his horror, that his wife had tried many times, and with many different poisons, to kill the man she had hated so bitterly.

He heard that salt had never been put in Overbury's food, for white arsenic had taken its place; that cantharides had been used instead of pepper, while a caustic poison called Lapis Costitus, together with powder of diamonds and a red arsenic called rosalgar, had all been given the wretched prisoner in his meals.

"It was Anne Turner who procured the

poisons!" sobbed Frances. "She gave the bribes, she — "

"My Lady," interrupted Sir Ralph, shaking his head, "you know very well that Mrs. Turner did what you paid her to do. It was you who wanted Overbury dead and yours was the hand behind it all."

Her tear-wet eyes flashed with a sudden defiance. "I wanted him out of the way!" she cried recklessly. "He was coming between Robbie and me! He hated me — hated me, I tell you!" She glanced for confirmation at her husband who closed his eyes and turned his head away. "He would have stopped our marriage — oh yes he would, for he knew I was not virgin, and he would have spoken out at the nullity hearing in order to stop it," she continued boldly. "I had to silence him. He would have ruined all our plans!"

"Oh my good God!" muttered Robert, half-inaudibly through clenched teeth, passing a trembling hand over his eyes. He drew a hard sobbing breath.

At once she turned to him, stretching out her hands imploringly.

"Robbie, Robbie — it was for you! I

did it all for you, Robbie! I love you so; I have loved you ever since you fell from your horse at the King's Tournament eight years ago. It was all for you, Robbie darling, it was all for you!"

He stared at her in terrible silence, his ravaged face working, unable to utter a word. She cried his name, besought him to speak to her, to look at her, sobbing over and over again that she loved him. A spasm passed across his face and he gave an involuntary shudder.

"And you are to bear my child," he said in a strangled voice, as though the words choked him. "Better for it if it were to die at birth, than be born of such a mother as you."

Disregarding her shriek of anguish, he rose to his feet and walked out of the room, tottering like an old man, or as one dealt a mortal wound.

9

SHE THAT DIGS A PIT
SHALL FALL INTO IT.

Told by Dorothy Badby.

I AM but a woman of low degree and have no courtly speech in which to recount happenings, but I will do my best to tell of what befell when the King's Commissioners came to call at Greys Court one autumn morning in 1615. My faith, there was a desperate garboil of crying, screaming, shouting and roaring enacted on that day and for long, long after too! It all came about because of the death of Sir Thomas Overbury who had perished in the Tower of London some two years before. My master and mistress, the Earl and Countess of Somerset, were staying at Greys Court with Lord and Lady Knollys. Lady Knollys being blood sister to my mistress and both very fond.

My Lord and Lady Somerset were thought to have some knowledge of the death of Sir Thomas Overbury — more than mere knowledge, indeed — and were forthwith placed under arrest by the Commissioners, which was a great and terrible shock to everyone, for who would have believed or thought of such a dreadful thing? Lord and Lady Knollys were utterly forstraught, hardly able to credit that their relatives should be in such fearful case. Lady Knollys, she fainted away and I do not wonder at it; his Lordship walked about, shaking his head and saying: "It cannot be true, it cannot be true!" again and again, while the servants were all in confusion, scarce knowing what they were about, or what to do next.

Anyhap, my Lord of Somerset and my Lady were hustled off to Henley, with no time to pack, surrounded by soldiers. I went with my Lady, for she would need a tiring-woman wherever she might go, and I will tell you that it was a mighty unpleasant sensation to be taken off, all sudden, like a criminal. My Lord was on horseback, seeming to be struck dumb, which was no surprise after the shock he had received. My Lady went in a litter, being pregnant, while that doxy of an Anne Turner rode, hands bound, pillion behind a soldier screaming nigh all the way to Henley, where we took water for London, it being easier for my Lady that way.

That Turner, she screamed most of the night at Maidenhead, where we rested, so I got no wink of sleep because of her fantods, and the same at Staines where we stayed another night. I thought her throat could not have stood up to all the yelling, but her voice-box must have been made of brass. She had good reason for her hollerings, mind you, for having confessed all her doings, she would surely hang for her wicked work as she was well aware! Even so, I was not best pleased to be kept awake when I needed my sleep, for I had need of my wits to equal to the managing of my Lady, who was in a rare state herself and near her time, withal.

When the boats tied up at Westminster, my Lord was taken away by Sir Oliver St. John to the Dean's house, there to remain under arrest, while my Lady and I were rowed down river to a house she owned at Blackfriars, to stay there as prisoners, forbidden to step outside, even into the gardens. Anne Turner was haled off to the Tower and what happened to her there I know not, except that she was hanged the next month, in November.

I heard that she went to her hanging all rouged and painted, her hair in curls, her gown of black satin richly ornamented with lace that was all coloured bright yellow with her famous starch. 'Twas no surprise to me to learn that after her death, yellow starch fell out of favour as fast as it had formerly fallen in. Everyone hated it as fierce as one of her own poisons after that!

Richard Weston, that wicked under-keeper, was hanged too and rightly so. Also strung up was James Franklin, the apothecary who had given Mrs. Turner several horrid poisons. I thought it a shame about Sir Gervase Elwys, though, for he was executed on the 20th of November and to me it seemed right unjust that he should be chopped when it seemed that he had done but little that was wrong. Even my Lady thought so.

"Why," she said, "that man saved Overbury's life many and many a time! For my part, I wish he had not, but he is killed because he kept silent." She paused, thinking of it. "Dost think I shall be 'headed, Dorothy?"

What a question to put to a servant! Well, I am one who blurts out what is in my head, for good or ill, so I said: "Murder is a 'heading matter, my Lady. You had best pray."

"Oh me!" she cried. "You are cold comfort! I am only twenty-three. Sure they will think me too young to die so."

I was not so sure. "There was one Lady Jane Grey who was executed in the last century," I said, "and she was but sixteen. My old granny used to tell me of it as her Mam told her. Being so young did not save the Lady Jane."

She slapped my face for that. As I said, I am no courtier. My tongue has a will of its own. And mark you, in all her troubles, my Lady said no word about the babe that was to come, poor mite. I doubt she gave it a thought.

It was because of the little one in her

womb that she had not yet been brought to trial, nor my Lord, neither. It was deemed best to delay until after the birth, which took place in early December, with a lovely little red-haired girl coming into the world with a murderess for a mother and a father held on suspicion of the same. No happy beginning to a life, to my mind. The babe would need more than a little good fortune to overcome such a start.

Well, my Lady came through the birth well enough, although it was a hard one and long. I assisted her, having helped at many a labour, for all that I am not a mother, nor even a wife. I never fancied marriage. I have seen too oft of its miseries and think to myself that men bring more woe than merriment in the end.

But be that as it may, once my selfish, self-willed lady had held her tiny red-haired nursling in her arms and to her breast, she opened her heart to the babe. She may even have made a good mother, for all I know, but she had already chosen her road and must needs follow it, come what might.

"Dorothy," she said to me one day, "here is my poor, sweet little child — Robbie's child, Doll. See, she has his hair and his beauty. Hearken to me now, Doll, and mark well what I say. Do you give an eye to her — promise me! Take her to my family, beseech them to care for her. Promise me, Dorothy — swear you will!"

And so I swore and so I did keep my promise in the years that followed. To do my Lady justice, she wept and suffered and yearned for her little Anne long after the child was taken from her. The babe was half her adored husband's, you see, and doubly precious to her because of that. And she pined for Lord Somerset very greatly, weeping much and full of fear that she had lost his love.

"Oh, how he looked at me when we parted!" she exclaimed one day. "I cannot forget it, such a look as it was. I felt that I had murdered him in some way, as well as that snake of an Overbury. Dost think he still loves me, Dorothy? Dost think he has forgiven me?"

"How can I tell my Lady?" said I. "Best to hope that he has forgiven you and trust in God that it be so."

"But love?" she cried. "What of love? Might he turn from me, think you? He said no word of farewell when we parted. Dost think he loves me still?"

I stared at her, having no answer. Myself, I doubted if he still loved her, for she was not in any way as he had thought her. I fancied he had surely turned from her, so heartless as he had discovered her to be. She loved him, ay, but in what fashion! To murder a man she felt would stand in her way — nay, that is not love, that is greed and ruthlessness. I thought she had killed my Lord's love as dead as she had killed poor Sir Thomas Overbury. Mind you, she never ceased to swear his innocence to all who came to question her.

"Lord Somerset had naught to do with it," she would maintain stoutly. "He knew naught of what I was about. It was all my own notion — none of his in any way. I am the guilty one and you must believe it."

But they did not believe it. They thought her to be shielding him, finding it hard to imagine that so beautiful and nobly-born a young lady could have wrought such evil out of her own mind. They thought my Lord must have known of it, but she denied it flatly and continued to do so all along.

"They may question me till they are black in the face," she said to me on a day in February. It was rare cold out, with the Thames like to be frozen over, so far as I could tell, all grey, with the snow clouds hanging low in the sky and the wind piercing through the panelling like a sword-blade to make the hangings shake and tremble. My Lady, sitting huddled by a great fire in the winter parlour that looked out over the gardens and the river, had called for a shawl, as the draughts were blowing down her back, despite the high back of the settle that she had chosen for a seat.

"The Commissioners keep plaguing me," she went on as I settled the shawl about her shoulders, "but I can only say that my Lord is innocent, because that is what he is! I shall be 'prisoned further, I know, but he should be set free, Dorothy. I wonder how long I must tarry before I am brought to trial? I wonder why it takes so long? The Commissioners possess all the evidence and I have borne my sweet babe, which was the reason for the delay."

I must have looked knowledgeable, for she rounded on me at once. "You know something, Doll! I can see by your face. Come, what is it? Pray tell me — pray do!"

To tell it could do no harm, so I spoke up. "We servants hear a great deal that you do not, my Lady, and I daresay the Commissioner gents would keep it from you, anyhap. The trial is delayed because of my Lord, your husband."

"Oh Jesu!" she cried, clasping her hands in fright. "Is he ill? Has he tried to escape? What is it?"

"He will not admit any guilt, my Lady, no matter how the Commissioners put him to the question."

"Oh Jesu!" she cried again. "He is not tortured, is he?"

"The King forbade that," I answered. "I heard Sir Fulke Greville say as much to Sir Ralph Winwood when they were here. He is too stubborn for their liking, see'st thou, and will not give in."

229

"And nor should he," she declared, "for he has done no wrong! I would not tell him of any of my plans, for he was greatly fond of Overbury and I would have lost him, sure, if he had guessed what I was about. Doll, sit down here — on this stool by me and talk with me as a friend. I have none now that my sweet Turner is gone to heaven."

I sat as she bade me. Her sweet Turner, indeed! That Anne Turner was about as sweet as the poisons she had bought and made! And as to heaven, there'd be none of it for her, I'd be ready to wager a ducat. It would be Satan and his imps, rather! It was Turner who had led my Lady into bad ways from the beginning — not that she had needed much urging, for an apt pupil in wrongdoing she became, to her cost. As ever, I burst out what was in my mind, all rough and graceless as is my way.

"Your sweet Turner was your worst enemy, my Lady, and heaven is not where she has gone, you may be sure."

"Oh, but she helped to rid me of Lord Essex, Dorothy. 'Twas she who kept his manhood down. She gave me the potions to do so."

Well, I had not known that, nor had anyone else except those she had dealt with in it. "Blessed Saint Mary!" I cried. "Was that her doing? Ah, it surprises me not. It was a bad course to take, my Lady, and you know it. You should have had naught to do with the woman."

"Ay, but Dorothy, I had known her near all my life and she was the only one who would help me."

"I never liked her," I said, shaking my head. "Never. She was too worldly wise, too quick, too conniving. Why could you not have stayed with Lord Essex? He seemed a pleasant enough young gentleman."

"Oh Doll, you *know* why I could not! I had fallen in love with my dear lord before Lord Essex ever came home. I did not want to be only my darling Robbie's mistress. I wanted to be his wife."

"But we cannot have all we want in this world," said I, trying to make her understand. "Not all the time, anyway. My Lady, you used potions upon my Lord of Essex which might have killed him, no matter what Mrs. Turner may have told you — and you did mean to kill Sir Thomas Overbury."

"Yes, I did," she replied quite coolly. "He would have spoilt my life."

"But is it not spoiled now?" I asked.

She opened her grey eyes wide. "I married my Robbie, did I not? I have had him for two years and borne his child, have I not? I would not have had any of that, had I not removed Overbury."

I was dumbfounded into silence at her words. It seemed that she knew not right from wrong.

"But you may be condemned to death, my Lady!" I exclaimed at last. "And Lord Somerset, too. Have you not thought of this?"

She looked thoughtful, then she smiled. "Oh, sure, he will not be condemned," she maintained. "I told you, he knew naught and as for me, why, the King will step in, I daresay."

"But if he does not?"

A frown grew between her level golden brows. "Oh, but he must," she said. "I am Frances Howard."

I gave it up. What could one do against such relentless vanity and self-interest? She had no conscience at all. There she sat, in her dark green velvet gown banded with sable, her pretty babe in a cradle beside her, for the little thing was still with her at that time; there she sat, looking as beautiful and pure as an angel, and she with a heart of sin as black as night! I tell you, I crossed my fingers and whispered a quick prayer to St. Anne for protection, for who knew that she had not the Evil Eye, so deep was she dyed in wickedness?

I was sorry for Lord Somerset and the babe. Sorry, too, in a way, for my Lady, for I was quite sure that she had lost his love. I, too, had seen his face when he was taken off to the Dean of Westminster's house. Oh, very well had I marked it! She had called a most loving and heartening farewell to him, bidding him not to fret, for he was innocent, and saying that she loved him more than anything in the wide world. He had answered no word; no Godspeed, no wishes for her health during her labour and no kind thoughts for the coming babe. He had merely turned slightly, staring over her head, his face blank except for a little twist to his mouth, as if he felt a faint nausea. Then he had ridden away with his escort and was gone.

Suddenly my Lady leaned toward me. "Dorothy," she said, "even if my darling has turned from me and loves me no more, I would do it all again."

I must have looked shocked, for she repeated her words. "I would do it all again, truly. I regret nothing. It was worth it, Doll, even if I do go to the block for it. My husband is more to me than life. I cannot live without him."

Ha, thought I, I wonder if you will say that if you are condemned to execution! Your fine-sounding words may moderate a little then, my Lady. 'Tis all very well to assert that you cannot live without the love of another when you have not been condemned! I daresay there have been some remarkable changes of mind when on the scaffold with the block and the axe in full view.

Well, the trial did not take place until the May of that year of 1616 as it turned out, and this was only because of my Lord's refusal to plead guilty to the murder. No reason to do so, I considered, if he were truly innocent. Of course, it was his enemies, of whom he had many, who wanted him sped, poor gentleman. He was hated, you understand. He could never seem to comprehend quite why he was so disliked, or how much, for I believe that his headpiece was not oversharp. Poor farmer's daughter though I be, I have more in my noddle than the great Earl of Somerset, I fancy! Why, I can read and make shift to write a letter too, although I do not brag of this for it would not be seemly in a mere tirewoman.

My education came about in this wise. I was taken into my Lord of Suffolk's household when I was but fourteen and one of his clerks had the whim to teach me my letters and such. He taught me other things too, of which I was all too apt a pupil. Then, when I fell pregnant, he left me for another, prettier wench. My baby died, which was a blessing, both for me and the child — it was a bad time. However, it so happened that my Lady Frances was born at much the same time as I lost my bastard babe, so I was kept on as a milk-woman and later as one of her nursemaids, and after that it was discovered that I had some skill in the management of gowns and articles of attire and I became personal tirewoman to my Lady, so I have always had a feeling for her. Not love, nor even much respect, but a sort of irritated concern that would not allow me to leave her. Yet of what good was my concern, when all was said and done? She fell under an evil influence and went down a wicked path, despite all. It was in her stars, I believe, that her fate was sealed and there was naught anyone could do to hinder it.

And here am I philosophising when I should be telling about the trial! I had ever the gift of the gab, I fear . . .

Well, in March 1616 my Lady Frances and Lord Somerset were taken to the Tower and there held captive. It was the first time that they had laid eyes on one another since the day of their arrival in London some five months earlier and, mercy upon me, what a falling out there was! Shouts, shrieks, sobs, accusations, excuses, protestations, recriminations — oh Word of God, a mighty to-do! My Lord's eyes were opened at last, you see, and he roared that he could not endure the sight of my Lady and wished to have no more to do with her, that his love had been built on a fantasy and now was as dead as a coffin-nail. He was finished with her for evermore, he bawled, his voice breaking on a half-sob as he shouted.

And she? Oh, I verily believe her hard heart broke, for she was quite bowed down that he should turn from her and she wept as I had never seen her weep in all her greedy, selfish life. She wept for days and nights together, constantly visiting his chamber, only to find the door bolted against her. She would pound upon it with her fists, wailing, sobbing, beseeching, falling to her knees, to her face, outside the door, but he would not open, nor even reply. It was pathetic to witness, if one did not recall what she had done, but to my mind it was but justice and richly deserved.

My Lord and Lady were not lodged unpleasantly while in the Tower. They had good rooms, comfortable furnishings and servants to wait upon them, but it was prison, nonetheless. The doors were locked at night and no walking outside was allowed. It chafed upon their sprits greatly, so that my Lady was almost relieved when the day of her trial came on the 24th of May.

I helped her to dress. We chose an elegant black silk gown, banded with black velvet over a petticoat, also of black, but with white embroidery upon it. With this, she wore a snow-white ruff and delicate white lawn cuffs, while I had arranged her hair high and full in curls. Her only jewellery was her emerald betrothal ring and her gold wedding band. I will say she looked lovely, though sad, and no more like a murderess than an angel straight from heaven.

"I shall plead Guilty," she said. "Sir Francis Bacon has assured me that if I do, I shall be treated with consideration. I hope he may be right, for I do not want to die while there still may be hope that Robbie might yet love me again."

"Well, you *are* guilty, my Lady," said

I in my usual forthright fashion, "and everyone knows it, so I see no reason for you to plead otherwise, and why you should be treated with consideration for doing so is more than I can make out!" And how she could hope for my Lord's love after the rejection she had suffered was also more than I could make out, but she was ever one to close her eyes to what she did not wish to see.

"Well, Robbie will not plead Guilty, I know, so I pray that all will go well for him," she said. "And do you pray for me, Dorothy, I beg you."

"I will, my Lady," I made answer. "I shall pray that you be not condemned."

She thanked me for that and we went to the trial. My oath, but there were a-many Lordships seated there! I saw my Lords of Worcester, Pembroke, Hertford, Montgomery, Rutland and Delaware ranged about and, of course, the Lords Commissioners. I cannot recall more names. None were friends of my Lord and my Lady, though, and right fierce did they all look, moreover.

Sir Francis Bacon made a fine speech, all against my Lady, to be sure, but what else could anyone say? Everyone knew of her crimes — they were no longer any secret. But Sir Francis did tell of the King's merciful nature and how he had never caused noble blood to be shed, not even the blood of noble traitors, so mayhap she had a chance, I thought.

When she was asked: "Prisoner, how do you plead?" she answered: "Guilty;" in a small clear voice. And then Lord Ellesmere spoke up in deep, melancholy tones that sent a shiver down my back.

"Frances, Countess of Somerset," he said, slow and terrible, "you are sentenced to death by this court, that your head may be struck from your body at what time the King's pleasure may decide and may the Lord have mercy on your soul."

Well, it was a shock, I will own it. My Lady trembled, her cheeks blanched under the rouge I had applied to disguise her prison pallor, and she pressed a hand to her bosom as if short of breath. I was afeared she would faint, but she did not, not she! As we left the courtroom with the blade of the executioner's axe was turned towards her, Sir Francis Bacon came forward.

"Have no fear, Lady Somerset," he told her. "His Majesty will spare you, as you will discover. You will not die and you will be pardoned, even as I said."

And so it fell out. My Lady received a royal pardon later in the year, but my Lord, though innocent, so far as anyone could tell, was not so fortunate. No matter what transpired, he refused to admit to any guilt and who could blame him, for who wishes to confess to a murder that one has not committed, or even known of? But his resistance was all of no use, for at his trial he was condemned, as had been my Lady, but no pardon was forthcoming. It was some months later, after Christmas of that year that he told me that those at his trial had been all his sworn enemies, so much so that he thought they must have been chosen especially; that they had no interest in his own speech of defence, but only to find him guilty whatever was said in his favour. Then, when his wife received her pardon and he did not, he realised that His Majesty, who had had the ordering of all, was done with him for ever.

What times, what times, when the innocent are pronounced guilty and the guilty are given a pardon! By my faith, it was almost a jest, though a grim one. I could scarce believe it, but there, it was so. Both my Lord and my Lady were thus allowed to live, but what a life, for they remained in the Tower for several long, weary years. Oh, it was ingenious punishment and worthy of the King's subtle brain, for he hated to kill and those two had been very dear to him in their time, in spite of the fact that he never wished to see their faces more.

I did not remain in the Tower with my master and mistress all the time, for my Lady sent me back and forth to her kinsfolk to see her child and bring her news of the little Lady Anne Carr. She fretted for the babe, sure enough, but her sorrow over this was as nothing to the agony she suffered over my Lord's utter rejection of her. Better she had been 'headed, she wept to me a thousand times, than to have to endure his loathing, for now he hated her as much as he had formerly idolised her, shouting and swearing at her and wishing that he had never laid eyes upon her. When he learned, through gossip and whisperings, that she had used potions upon himself, he went near wild.

"Doxy! Harlot! Filthy, murdering whore!" I heard him yell at her. "You are the devil's daughter — a curst witch! You sicken me. Get you from my sight, for you are dead to me — dead, I say! Take your hands off me and get away!" Shoving her roughly aside, so that she fell, wailing and sobbing to the floor, he strode off to his rooms.

He never spoke to her again.

★ ★ ★

It was during the cold, grey month of January, five years and eight months later, that they were released at last. She was then in her twenty-ninth year, looking very much older, thin and sickly, with her once bright hair now dull and straw-like, her eyes hollow and shadowed and lines of abiding grief etched upon her face from which the look of youth and confidence had long since fled. He had now almost thirty-six years, and I swear to you that anyone would have taken him for ten years the more. I never saw a man so aged and hopeless looking, his fine shoulders sagging, his face deeply lined, drawn and sad. For all that, his bonny red hair was as bright and waving as ever and he was still right good to look upon, for he had the kind of face which only improves with age, seeming to defy the ravages of time and illness, gaining in refinement and dignity by some mysterious alchemy. Ay, five years and more of imprisonment had taken its toll and, although they had been allowed visitors and dainty food in the Tower, it was not freedom.

And even upon their release they were not free, for they were given the choice of but two residences. These were the two houses of Lord Knollys; Greys Court in Oxfordshire, and another in Caversham, some few miles away, over the county boundary in Berkshire. Lord Knollys had recently been created Viscount Wallingford by the King, perhaps as a sop to the inconvenience of having one of his homes permanently occupied by others! There was some discussion over the choice and the new Lord Wallingford decided to allow my Lord and my Lady to have Greys Court, it being smaller than his house at Caversham. My Lord of Somerset looked to have his earldom taken from him, but the King allowed him to retain it, together with his George of the Order of the Garter, in memory of happier days, which was some sort of kindness and hardly expected. As it was, his life was wretched enough, he being permitted to ride abroad no more than three miles in any direction and my Lady the same.

Oftentimes he would saddle a horse and gallop off, wild as though pursued by devils instead of only his guards, but to what purpose? He could go nowhere, only to Henley, that small riverside village of a few hundred souls, or to Checkendon, Stoke How, Nettlebed or Nutfield, these being naught but tiny hamlets only. With nowhere to go, little to do, no friends, no wife that he would admit to or acknowledge and constantly overwatched by guards, his life was a desert indeed.

My Lady, heart-sunk and spiritless, seldom ventured further than the castle ruins, some fifty yards from the northern front of the house. There she would walk, pale, silent and weary, ever longing for my Lord who spurned her. Sometimes, but rarely, she would choose the small formal garden on the south side, with its pretty flower beds, gay and bright in summer, neat and well-kept in winter.

"Yet I prefer the ruins, Dorothy," she would sigh. "Their dilapidated towers and broken walls remind me of my wrecked life and my lost beauty."

"A miserable conceit, my Lady," I would rally her. "Sure, you must take heart, or heaviness of spirit will overcome you."

But she would have none of that.

"Take heart?" she would ask sadly. "Ah, how can I? My heart is broke and will not mend. My husband wants me not, my child is taken from me and I am a prisoner here till my life's end. And I wish that time would come, Doll. I wish it would come. I would I might die now and be out of my misery."

But she had to wait long for her ending and when it came, it was not easy, but drawn-out, difficult and agonising.

I tended her. I could do no less after we had gone through so much together, besides which, the child, Lady Anne Carr, would run to me when I visited her and send messages through me to the parents she had never seen. After my Lady's sad and painful death the Lady Anne was given leave to visit her father, she being seventeen years old by then and soon to wed.

On her deathbed, my Lady drew from me a promise to go to the Lady Anne and beg to be allowed to serve her and this I did. The pretty sweeting had heard somewhat of her parents doings, over the years, of course. Children have sharp ears and folk will gossip, be they never so discreet, so I said as little as I could to her of her mother, but told her that she looked very like her father who had been as handsome as a god in his young days, he who had been more sinned against than sinning and who longed above all things to lay eyes upon her, his only child. And in the end, permission was given, so that my sorrowful, unlucky Lord's broken heart healed just a little.

I am old myself now, being full

seventy-two years of age. Sure, I cannot last much longer, so ancient am I! My Lord of Somerset died, scarce noticed, some seven years back, unmourned but for the Lady Anne and me. He was fifty-nine then, white-haired, still fine-looking, but weary of a life that had dragged on for too long in lonely sadness. His end was quiet and peaceful, for it was in his sleep that his grieving heart ceased to beat.

I pray that God received him and that his soul rests in peace.

Authors' Note.

1. Robert Carr, disgraced Earl of Somerset, died in 1645 in the year of the Battle of Naseby during the Civil War. Charles I, son of James I, was then King.

2. Greys Court still appears much the same externally as it did in 1600, except that the three courtyards are gone, their place being taken by lawns and flower beds. The interior has been greatly altered over the centuries.

J.D.

Other titles in the
Ulverscroft Large Print Series:

TO FIGHT THE WILD
Rod Ansell and Rachel Percy

Lost in uncharted Australian bush, Rod Ansell survived by hunting and trapping wild animals, improvising shelter and using all the bushman's skills he knew.

COROMANDEL
Pat Barr

India in the 1830s is a hot, uncomfortable place, where the East India Company still rules. Amelia and her new husband find themselves caught up in the animosities which seethe between the old order and the new.

THE SMALL PARTY
Lillian Beckwith

A frightening journey to safety begins for Ruth and her small party as their island is caught up in the dangers of armed insurrection.

THE WILDERNESS WALK
Sheila Bishop

Stifling unpleasant memories of a misbegotten romance in Cleave with Lord Francis Aubrey, Lavinia goes on holiday there with her sister. The two women are thrust into a romantic intrigue involving none other than Lord Francis.

THE RELUCTANT GUEST
Rosalind Brett

Ann Calvert went to spend a month on a South African farm with Theo Borland and his sister. They both proved to be different from her first idea of them, and there was Storr Peterson — the most disturbing man she had ever met.

ONE ENCHANTED SUMMER
Anne Tedlock Brooks

A tale of mystery and romance and a girl who found both during one enchanted summer.

CLOUD OVER MALVERTON
Nancy Buckingham

Dulcie soon realises that something is seriously wrong at Malverton, and when violence strikes she is horrified to find herself under suspicion of murder.

AFTER THOUGHTS
Max Bygraves

The Cockney entertainer tells stories of his East End childhood, of his RAF days, and his post-war showbusiness successes and friendships with fellow comedians.

MOONLIGHT
AND MARCH ROSES
D. Y. Cameron

Lynn's search to trace a missing girl takes her to Spain, where she meets Clive Hendon. While untangling the situation, she untangles her emotions and decides on her own future.

NURSE ALICE IN LOVE
Theresa Charles

Accepting the post of nurse to little Fernie Sherrod, Alice Everton could not guess at the romance, suspense and danger which lay ahead at the Sherrod's isolated estate.

POIROT INVESTIGATES
Agatha Christie

Two things bind these eleven stories together — the brilliance and uncanny skill of the diminutive Belgian detective, and the stupidity of his Watson-like partner, Captain Hastings.

LET LOOSE THE TIGERS
Josephine Cox

Queenie promised to find the long-lost son of the frail, elderly murderess, Hannah Jason. But her enquiries threatened to unlock the cage where crucial secrets had long been held captive.

THE TWILIGHT MAN
Frank Gruber

Jim Rand lives alone in the California desert awaiting death. Into his hermit existence comes a teenage girl who blows both his past and his brief future wide open.

DOG IN THE DARK
Gerald Hammond

Jim Cunningham breeds and trains gun dogs, and his antagonism towards the devotees of show spaniels earns him many enemies. So when one of them is found murdered, the police are on his doorstep within hours.

THE RED KNIGHT
Geoffrey Moxon

When he finds himself a pawn on the chessboard of international espionage with his family in constant danger, Guy Trent becomes embroiled in moves and countermoves which may mean life or death for Western scientists.

TIGER TIGER
Frank Ryan

A young man involved in drugs is found murdered. This is the first event which will draw Detective Inspector Sandy Woodings into a whirlpool of murder and deceit.

CAROLINE MINUSCULE
Andrew Taylor

Caroline Minuscule, a medieval script, is the first clue to the whereabouts of a cache of diamonds. The search becomes a deadly kind of fairy story in which several murders have an other-worldly quality.

LONG CHAIN OF DEATH
Sarah Wolf

During the Second World War four American teenagers from the same town join the Army together. Forty-two years later, the son of one of the soldiers realises that someone is systematically wiping out the families of the four men.

THE LISTERDALE MYSTERY
Agatha Christie

Twelve short stories ranging from the light-hearted to the macabre, diverse mysteries ingeniously and plausibly contrived and convincingly unravelled.

TO BE LOVED
Lynne Collins

Andrew married the woman he had always loved despite the knowledge that Sarah married him for reasons of her own. So much heartache could have been avoided if only he had known how vital it was to be loved.

ACCUSED NURSE
Jane Converse

Paula found herself accused of a crime which could cost her her job, her nurse's reputation, and even the man she loved, unless the truth came to light.

A GREAT DELIVERANCE
Elizabeth George

Into the web of old houses and secrets of Keldale Valley comes Scotland Yard Inspector Thomas Lynley and his assistant to solve a particularly savage murder.

'E' IS FOR EVIDENCE
Sue Grafton

Kinsey Millhone was bogged down on a warehouse fire claim. It came as something of a shock when she was accused of being on the take. She'd been set up. Now she had a new client — herself.

A FAMILY OUTING IN AFRICA
Charles Hampton and Janie Hampton

A tale of a young family's journey through Central Africa by bus, train, river boat, lorry, wooden bicyle and foot.

THE PLEASURES OF AGE
Robert Morley

The author, British stage and screen star, now eighty, is enjoying the pleasures of age. He has drawn on his experiences to write this witty, entertaining and informative book.

THE VINEGAR SEED
Maureen Peters

The first book in a trilogy which follows the exploits of two sisters who leave Ireland in 1861 to seek their fortune in England.

A VERY PAROCHIAL MURDER
John Wainwright

A mugging in the genteel seaside town turned to murder when the victim died. Then the body of a young tearaway is washed ashore and Detective Inspector Lyle is determined that a second killing will not go unpunished.

DEATH ON A
HOT SUMMER NIGHT
Anne Infante

Micky Douglas is either accident-prone or someone is trying to kill him. He finds himself caught in a desperate race to save his ex-wife and others from a ruthless gang.

HOLD DOWN A SHADOW
Geoffrey Jenkins

Maluti Rider, with the help of four of the world's most wanted men, is determined to destroy the Katse Dam and release a killer flood.

THAT NICE MISS SMITH
Nigel Morland

A reconstruction and reassessment of the trial in 1857 of Madeleine Smith, who was acquitted by a verdict of Not Proven of poisoning her lover, Emile L'Angelier.

SEASONS OF MY LIFE
Hannah Hauxwell
and Barry Cockcroft

The story of Hannah Hauxwell's struggle to survive on a desolate farm in the Yorkshire Dales with little money, no electricity and no running water.

TAKING OVER
Shirley Lowe and Angela Ince

A witty insight into what happens when women take over in the boardroom and their husbands take over chores, children and chickenpox.

AFTER MIDNIGHT STORIES,
The Fourth Book Of

A collection of sixteen of the best of today's ghost stories, all different in style and approach but all combining to give the reader that special midnight shiver.

DEATH TRAIN
Robert Byrne

The tale of a freight train out of control and leaking a paralytic nerve gas that turns America's West into a scene of chemical catastrophe in which whole towns are rendered helpless.

THE ADVENTURE OF THE CHRISTMAS PUDDING
Agatha Christie

In the introduction to this short story collection the author wrote "This book of Christmas fare may be described as 'The Chef's Selection'. I am the Chef!"

RETURN TO BALANDRA
Grace Driver

Returning to her Caribbean island home, Suzanne looks forward to being with her parents again, but most of all she longs to see Wim van Branden, a coffee planter she has known all her life.

SKINWALKERS
Tony Hillerman

The peace of the land between the sacred mountains is shattered by three murders. Is a 'skinwalker', one who has rejected the harmony of the Navajo way, the murderer?

A PARTICULAR PLACE
Mary Hocking

How is Michael Hoath, newly arrived vicar of St. Hilary's, to meet the demands of his flock and his strained marriage? Further complications follow when he falls hopelessly in love with a married parishioner.

A MATTER OF MISCHIEF
Evelyn Hood

A saga of the weaving folk in 18th century Scotland. Physician Gavin Knox was desperately seeking a cure for the pox that ravaged the slums of Glasgow and Paisley, but his adored wife, Margaret, stood in the way.

SOUTH LANARKSHIRE LIBRARIES

HOUSEBOUND SERVICE

674		
625		
962		
wp		
1081		
206		
1153		
98		
SCH		
KNH		
1060		
WP		
VDC		